SO I MARRIED AN ALIEN

LYONNE RILEY

INTRODUCTION

What's a girl to do when her cat dies and a plague wipes out most of the male population? Why, she marries an alien, of course!

Amara is a party girl with a boring day job, in search of meaning in her life. When she applies to the Galactic Matching Program looking for an alien husband of her own, she's paired with Roth'kar, a four-armed Karthinian with adorable antennae. Four arms may present problems when it comes to buying new clothes, but Amara's excited to find out what else her new husband can do with them.

Roth'kar was raised in poverty on a ship in deep space, scrounging for enough to live. His plan to escape? The Matching Program, where all he has to do is please a human bride for thirty days to earn full residency on Earth, and then he'll be free to do as he pleases. Though the planet is overrun with strange, dangerous animals— spiders, disgusting!—Roth'kar can finally feel the sun on his skin.

But he didn't expect his new wife to be sweet and

thoughtful, teaching him the value of kissing, the thrill of clubbing, and the simple joy of a walk in the park. As Roth'kar falls for Amara, will his plans change?

CONTENT WARNINGS

May contain spoilers.

- Graphic depictions of sex
- Weird peen
- Alcohol use
- Drug use (marijuana)
- Double penetration
- Death of an animal (off-screen, as a memory)

CHAPTER ONE

AMARA

THE DAY I make the call to the matchmaker isn't too dissimilar from other days, but it is the three-month anniversary of the death of my cat, Elvis. It seems that was the last straw.

I'm tired of being alone. Finding a male partner on Earth is difficult, if not impossible, since RVS blew through our society, and nearly two billion men were wiped off the face of the planet in a matter of months.

Believe me when I say I did try dating other women, but it wasn't for me.

There aren't a lot of options, then, if a man is what you're after. Most people who want one simply remain, well, partnerless. Very few even consider the Galactic Matching Program. My friends certainly gave me the side-eye when I mentioned it.

This keeps me from placing the call for a while. What would Marguerite and Fiona think when they found out? I know they'd judge me for being "desperate." But what's a girl to do when her cat dies and she feels like she has nothing left anchoring her to life?

Well, she calls up the alien matchmaker, that's what she does.

The female-sounding voice on the other end is nice enough once she gets her translator working properly. I don't have one, but she promises that my future husband, should I get approved, will come with his own and should have no trouble communicating with me.

I can't believe I'm doing this.

They send me a long questionnaire, which I fill out as truthfully as possible. It asks some very invasive questions about my sex life, and I'm forced to admit that it's basically non-existent. I have a very reliable dildo.

There are also questions about my work, how I spend my time off, my hobbies, and my preferred sleeping hours.

Once it's submitted, I wait.

And wait.

And wait.

I go to the office every day, and come home every night, wondering when I'm going to hear back. I still haven't told my friends about applying. I won't unless I have to.

And then, after two months have trudged by, I get a call from an unrecognized number. I answer it quickly, as I have every spam call I've received since sending in my application.

"Greetings, Amara Costin. This transmission is to let you know that your application for the Galactic Matching Program has been accepted. Please wait for further instructions."

A few moments later, a real person gets on the line. "Hello, Amara?"

Eagerly I answer, "Yes?"

"Your application has been approved. Roth'kar, who has been chosen for you, will arrive on Earth in three days, four hours, and thirty-two minutes. Please come early to fill out additional paperwork before your meeting time."

I jot everything down as fast as I can, including my new husband's ring size, and then the operator tells me goodbye without offering anything else.

Oh, god. I'm about to marry an alien.

They didn't mention that the husband they sent me has four arms. I feel like the number of arms is an important thing to bring up when pairing you with a potential life partner. Would the extra arms have made a difference if I had known? I'm not sure. Of course, I did sign up to marry an alien, so I expected some differences, but I've seen very few aliens in person.

Said extra arms are folded across his chest as we stand there on opposite sides of the dimly lit meeting room, the lower pair hanging at his sides. The arms aren't the most arresting thing about him, though. His skin is a bright bluish purple, like the night sky right after sunset. A pair of short stalks on his head twitch and bob as he regards me. Does he really have *antennae*?

In the next room, we'll get married, or so the match-maker said. It's really just a ceremony, and we won't sign the official papers until the thirty-day trial period is up—er, actually, I think we'll be using one of those fancy tablets all the aliens have.

Then we'll officially be husband and wife, and he will earn his full residency on Earth. If we make it that long.

I hope we do. All I truly want is a partner at the end of this. I think we can make it if he's here for the reason he says he is: to find forever. He must be, if he was willing to travel all this way just to be my husband.

I need someone as committed to this as I am. And I have to hope that the matchmaker knew what he was doing when he paired us up.

My groom is dressed in a smudged uniform that covers his shoulders and thighs, strapped around the middle with a belt. Underneath are a pair of loose leggings. It's the same sort of thing the matchmaker is wearing where he stands between us, and the same thing that most aliens who visit Earth wear.

The galaxy has very mid fashion sense.

Gazargo, the matchmaker, hops off the stool that keeps him at eye level with us. Now I have to peer down to look into his squat face.

"Roth'kar, this is Amara," Gazargo says, gesturing at each of us as he says our names. "Amara, this is Roth'kar."

I hold out a hand to shake, which seems like the polite thing to do with a stranger. Roth'kar stares down at my hand with his ethereal blue eyes, then back up at me. His odd antennae follow the track of his gaze.

Gazargo clears his throat. "They do not have handshakes in Karthinian culture," he tells me. "She is trying to greet you, Roth'kar. How do you do it where you come from?"

Roth'kar brings both pairs of hands to his chest, pressing his palms flat, then lifts his chin and closes his eyes.

"This is how we greet one another formally," he says in a deep, booming voice.

Wow, that voice is even stranger than his eyes. It's almost hollow, reverberating through my bones. I've never heard anything like it; it's as if he's playing an instrument.

I imitate his gesture, placing my hands on my chest and lifting my chin, and say, "It's good to meet you, Roth'kar."

The corner of his mouth tweaks upward. That's good. I think that's a smile, though I can't take anything for granted with an alien. Wish I'd gotten some kind of primer on his species before this so I didn't look like an idiot, but here we are.

"How are you speaking English?" I ask. "I thought you were going to have a translator, but it seems like you're fluent."

He gives me a perplexed look. "I do have a translator." He taps his temple. "It's been implanted here, so I can communicate with all Earthlings."

My mouth bobs open and closed. It's inside his *brain?* Okay, that's wicked cool and also kind of scary.

"It won't catch everything, but most of it," Gazargo interjects. "And it can provide Roth'kar some cultural context to help him adapt."

I stare at them both. "Neat." Maybe that's why his voice sounds so strange and otherworldly.

"Now that you've met, let's get on with the ceremony." Gazargo waddles away to the adjoining room, and Roth'kar and I reach it at the same time. He nods at me to walk through the door first and holds it open. Up close, I realize how tall he is, almost whole head higher than I am, and I'm a fairly tall girl.

On the other side of the door is yet another dimly lit room, this time with a small window looking out onto the docking bay. This is where spaceships come and go, a port that was built not long after first contact was made.

The first aliens we met were all like Gazargo—small, gray, and kind of wrinkled with a face like a turtle. They'd gotten a permit from the Intergalactic Association of Civilizations to make contact with us so they could try to sell us... well, *stuff*.

Those aliens, the Frahma, opened the door for other alien species to take note of us. We had a unique plight here on Earth after the RVS plague, one that called for out-of-towners to be imported to fill the need. And so eventually, Gazargo established his matchmaking service.

That's what the Frahma are good at. I think they could figure out a way to sell you your own clothes.

Gazargo leads us to a pedestal, pointing to each of us and then to either side of it.

"You, stand there." Then he climbs up steps on the back until he's about eye level with us and pulls out a tablet to read. "On this day, the third of October, in this year of twenty twenty-nine, I hereby match Amara Costin, with Roth'kar, the Fifth of His Name. These two will join in matrimony, to build a home together, and—"

As the words go on and on, other thoughts float up to the surface. Roth'kar isn't looking at me. He's glaring intently at Gazargo, as if willing him to get to the end of his spiel faster. At least we have that in common. I want this to be over just as much so we can get on with our future life.

I was so excited about this, so ready to finally have a companion and a chance to fall in love, but now that I'm seeing Roth'kar with my own eyes—all four arms of him —I'm second-guessing myself. Is it just my imagination, or does he not look happy to be here? I know nothing about Karthinians, so I'm going to have to start from scratch. I knew we'd have differences, of course, but I'd hoped my new husband would be a little more... excited.

Perhaps it's just cultural. I'll find out soon.

I got a futon for my office, since we don't know each other yet and inviting a strange alien into my bed seemed like we'd be moving a little fast. But thinking about it now, I'm sure the futon won't be big enough for Roth'kar. I'll have to trade with him and sleep on it myself while he has my bed.

"Amara?" Gazargo asks, startling me out of my thoughts. "It's time?"

Time for what? I search my mind for what's involved in a wedding ceremony.

"Oh! Right." I had rings made for us. The one thing the matchmaker *did* give me was Roth'kar's ring size. I pull out the box and remove both rings, plain but plated with gold, which earns a curious look from Roth'kar's freakishly blue eyes.

"What are these?" he asks, peering closer at them.

"It's an Earth tradition, one of them," Gazargo says, plucking my ring from my palm and giving it to my new alien groom. "Now put the ring on her hand, Roth'kar."

Roth'kar grunts, never looking up at me as he reaches

for my hand. At least he only has five fingers. I don't know how I'd handle six or seven on top of the double arms.

Carefully, Roth'kar slides the ring onto one of my fingers—the index one.

"Wrong finger," I say gently, then wiggle my ring finger. "It goes on that one."

With a huff of impatience, Roth'kar does as I tell him, removing the ring and then plunking it onto my ring finger instead. He pulls away, and the band shines in the low light.

"Your turn," Gazargo says to him.

Roth'kar holds out his lower hand for me—I'm glad he chose an arm himself, as I only brought one ring—and I slip the ring onto his ring finger, pushing the band down until it's seated.

When I stand up straight again, Roth'kar is pointedly looking away from me, his cheeks stained a dark bluish color. He retracts his hand, flexing his fingers before returning them to his side along with, well, his other hand.

Gosh, so many hands.

Then an unbidden thought hops into my brain. If he has two sets of arms... does he also have two—?

I can't think like that. We're still strangers. It will take time for us to get to know each other, which we'll have to do before any funny business can happen.

"And now, you say your commitments," Gazargo instructs.

"Commitments?" Roth'kar's brow pinches. "I am committed now."

"Yes, yes, they are just nice things to say before you

agree to the marriage." Gazargo waves a hand dismissively. "Come up with something."

"I'll go first," I interject, because I actually wrote something down and rehearsed it at home. "Roth'kar. I promise I will be honest with you, sometimes even when you don't want to hear it. I promise to be loyal to you, unless it's at a game of Bullshit. I promise to cherish you, and to have no others, until death do us part."

Roth'kar's mouth drops open.

"Until death do us part?" he repeats, horrified.

"It's a common phrase in human matrimony," Gazargo says. "Now, yours, Roth'kar."

The alien flexes his throat like he wants to speak, but all the words he had are gone.

"Uh," he says, then curses something in his own tongue that his translator must not be able to translate. "I will also, erm, cherish you, and be loyal to you." He doesn't mention anything about honesty. "I will do all my due diligences as your husband, as they are called for."

What? *As they are called for?* Well, at least he seems dedicated to his responsibilities, whatever he thinks those are. That's a good sign.

"Oh, all right." I smile brightly. "That's nice, thank you."

"Do you take Roth'kar to be your lawful husband?" Gazargo asks me.

I nod. This is what I signed up for, after all. "I do."

"And do you, Roth'kar, take Amara to be your lawful wife?"

Those glowing eyes settle on my face, and I wonder who he is under that indifferent expression and if he'll show me.

Eventually, he nods and says, "I do."

CHAPTER TWO

ROTH'KAR

WHAT DO THESE RINGS SYMBOLIZE? I am still pondering this even as we say our commitments, and then once again confirm that we have, in fact, chosen to be married. Why did I have to say it three times in three different ways?

Lower-class Karthinian mating rituals are much simpler. You agree to be a union and then live out that union—without all this pomp and circumstance. We do not have the luxuries of rings and ceremonies in the Hole.

Adapting to human culture will likely involve a lot of change and learning for me. Amara is an odd creature, besides the two arms. Her face is an appealing shape with high cheekbones and a pointed chin, and she has huge dark eyes. I have never seen a being that looks like her before, with voluminous wavy brown hair cascading down her back.

I would not have made such a wild decision as

bringing home a stranger, were I in her position. In fact, I would be happy to live alone if I had the money and means to do so. But when the Galactic Matching Program opened, I realized it was the only way I could escape *New Dro'thar II* in my natural life.

Once the idea was put into my head of getting off our ship, of leaving behind the scrap metal and the dirty water and constant struggle, I couldn't shake the thought. I couldn't bear an entire life lived in the dark underbelly of *New Dro'thar II* with UV lights glaring down from overhead in the few "sun" rooms. Even just this glimpse out the window at the port steals my attention.

What is beyond? As we flew in this morning, the landscape from overhead took my breath away. Earth is strange and yet lovely, covered in a green color I've never witnessed in such great quantities.

I wonder if you can eat it.

"Roth'kar," Gazargo says, "it's time to sign the agreement to the thirty-day trial period."

Both Amara and I write our names on the tablet, and then it's finished. I look forward to returning in thirty days and getting my official residency on Earth, so I can leave all this silliness behind me.

"Now, should anything come up, feel free to call." Gazargo fishes around in his pocket, withdrawing a communicator, and passes it to me. "We believe that we've matched the two of you well, but should there be a problem, let us know. We would like to try to mediate before resorting to separation."

I will give the human woman no reason to send me home. In fact, I could crush this communicator right now and that would solve the problem.

But I don't. I give the little Frahma an appreciative nod and tuck it away.

"Dang," says Amara under her breath. "I wanted a cool alien gadget."

Then, suddenly, we are done, and it's time for us to leave. For me to leave, with her, with this strange woman on this strange planet where I know none of the rules or customs.

Perhaps I should have studied humans a little before coming. There was just too much to do to get ready to leave, too many people I had to say goodbye to. I gave away what things I had left, rationing them out to those who needed them most, knowing I wouldn't require them anymore once I arrived on Earth.

That's the trade. Amara gets me, a "husband," and I get a new home on a planet that hasn't yet been consumed by greed—with all my needs taken care of. A life I could never have imagined for myself before that short, stubby alien showed up on our spaceship with a monstrous voice projector that enforcers had to fight to take away from him. He was so eagerly shouting about something called "Mexican food."

I follow Amara out another door into the spaceport, trailing behind her as we cross the crescent-moon-shaped dock. Even if we wanted to speak, we couldn't with the sound of engines roaring to life and ships arriving. But she does glance over her shoulder at me, shooting me an apologetic look.

"We're over here!" she shouts, loud enough my translator can pick it up. I nod in understanding and keep pace with her, carrying my one mostly empty bag.

We duck through yet another door and emerge from

the spaceport into a great field of black pavement. It's littered with ground-traveling vehicles, which stops me short.

"Wheels?" I ask, amazed. "Your vehicles still have wheels?" So the humans haven't even reached the point of hovercraft yet.

Amara appears perplexed. "Yes? What else would they have?"

I shake my head ruefully. I heard from friends that humans were not that advanced of a species, but I didn't realize the full extent of it.

"They would fly, obviously. Or hover. Wheels require roads, which are a terrible waste of space."

Amara gazes out at the sprawling parking lot, then taps her chin. "You're not wrong about that." She shrugs. "Oh well! No flying cars yet, so Toyota Corolla it is."

"Toyo-tah... what?"

She gestures for me to follow, so I do, eager to get to where we're going and perhaps have something to eat. They fed me during the journey, but it wasn't enough. After the number of meals I've skipped in my life, I devoured everything.

I hope Amara is prepared for a Karthinian's appetite. I hope that her food is better than *kath*, the protein bars we eat on *New Dro'thar II*.

We pass vehicle after vehicle until we reach a squat green one. Amara opens a door for me and gestures to get in, so I crouch and slide onto the gray fabric seat. Then she closes the door, locking me inside the small space.

She hops in on the other side and tosses her bag into the backseat carelessly. The vehicle's engine groans as it starts. Amara shoots me a nervous smile, then backs out of her parking spot, glancing over her shoulder.

Though we're navigating long stretches of pavement and creeping between tall buildings, all I can see is the *sky*. It's a marvelous bright blue, with dots of white clouds occasionally drifting over the single sun.

Real sun, not just UV lamps. As we take a turn, it hits my skin, warming me to the bone, and I close my eyes to drink it in.

"So, Roth'kar," Amara says, startling me. She nervously taps her steering wheel. "What are you most excited about on Earth?"

I stare at her. Most excited about? I am most excited about being on a planet, regardless of what planet it is. I am most excited about breathing fresh air. I am thrilled to have real earth under my feet.

Instead, I say, "The food." That's true enough. Karthinians and humans can digest the same types of proteins, so everything on this planet should be safe for me to eat. And if Amara is well-off enough in her society that she can bring an alien "husband" to her planet, she will have plenty of food.

"Oh?" Her thick brown eyebrows fly high on her forehead. Humans are so expressive, almost exaggeratedly so. When Amara smiles, it is a big, broad smile, the type of smile a Karthinian would save only for their closest loved ones. It's blinding. "What foods in particular?"

I fidget in my seat. "They didn't give me much information about Earth's culinary, um, delights."

Amara snaps one of her fingers. "They didn't tell me anything, either! Like, I didn't even know you were going to be a *Karnathawan*."

"Karthinian," I correct her.

"See?" Her eyes travel to me, and I urge her silently to look back at the road. "If I had known, I would have practiced my introductions and stuff."

I did know I was coming to Earth; I simply didn't spend the time looking into what that meant. Would I have changed my mind if I'd been aware they only have wheeled vehicles?

"It's not a problem," I say as she turns the car through an intersection with enough velocity that I have to hold on to the door. Honks fill the air, and a tire screeches. "We have plenty of time to learn about one another."

Right. I must assure her I'm in this for the long haul. I do not want to give her any reasons to end the trial. Once the thirty days are up and I am a permanent resident of Earth, then I will sort out the logistics.

"Aw, I like how you say that." Amara smiles at me again as she takes her eyes off the front window of the vehicle. Surely we're going to collide with another car. "You're really all-in, huh?"

"Yes." The lie burns my throat a little on the way out. I'm not a habitual liar, but I'll do what I have to do to survive, as I always did in the Hole. "Though I would be more comfortable if you look where you are going, seeing as there is no autopilot in this vehicle."

Agreeably, Amara turns back to the road. "Well, I have some food at home I can put together, or we can go out for dinner. But that might be a lot for you to take in on your first night."

Perhaps seeing her home today is enough for now. I want to get an idea of our living arrangements.

We are officially "husband and wife," and as a pair, I

believe it's expected that we will participate in sexual activities. Once I have a moment alone, I plan to find a guide on my communicator to learn quickly what I need to learn. Thanks to the Frahma, I'm aware that our species are compatible, but I know little more than that.

We cannot reproduce, though, given we are entirely different species. We are lucky to even have the same number of fingers.

"Eating at your home would be ideal," I say. "It was a long trip today."

"You're all worn out, huh?" Amara gives me another beaming smile. This must be a human idiosyncrasy, to give intimate smiles out like they mean nothing.

I am frightened of what her frown might look like. Does she shoot laser beams from her eyes?

Eventually the buildings give way, growing shorter and shorter, until suddenly, great walls of green appear to either side of the road. We're traveling fast now, along with many other wheeled vehicles. I'd have far greater anxiety about it if I weren't completely entranced with the view.

"What is this?" I ask, reaching out as if I could touch all the green.

"Trees?" Amara giggles. "Those are trees."

"They're so... green."

"Wait until we're deeper into autumn. Then they all change color at once, right before the leaves fall off."

I spin around in my seat. "Fall off?"

"Yes! The green stuff is the leaves on the trees. In the winter, the leaves change from green to yellow and orange, then they all die and fall off."

I screw up my lips, disturbed by all this talk of dying

among humans, and how it seems so common and regular to them that they would say *until death do us part*.

"The leaves grow back," Amara assures me when she sees my face. I beg her silently to look at the road. "Every spring."

"They die and regrow every year?" It seems laborious, when they could just grow once and leave it at that. "Why?"

Amara simply shrugs. "Who knows? That's just the cycle of life."

I sit back against the headrest, thinking this over. In my world, the cycle of life is to be born, to suffer for a while, and then to die. When you die, of course, you're ejected from the ship without a pod. They stopped giving out pods a long time ago unless you're one of the very wealthy.

Not even Earth is free of this inevitable destruction, I suppose. But at least it sounds beautiful on the way to death, and then there is this *spring* she mentioned, when it all comes back.

"I look forward to seeing it," I tell her, attempting a version of a smile.

This seems to please her immensely. "Good. You'll love it. And that time of year is Halloween—"

"Halloween?" I repeat, trying to commit this to memory. The more I know and understand about Earth, the easier it'll be for me to build a life here later.

"Oh, it's the *best* holiday," Amara says, brightening even more. This time she does, thankfully, keep her eyes on the road. "Everybody cuts open pumpkins and carves faces into them."

I hope that a "pumpkin" is not an animal of some

kind. My translator supplies some kind of large, awkward fruit.

"What do you do with these pumpkins? That seems like a waste."

"You put a candle in the pumpkin and then set it on your porch, so at night, it glows! Then you can see the scary face. Or happy face. Or whatever you want it to be. Some people do, like, really amazing pictures."

She talks so fast that even my translator has a hard time keeping up, blending her words together until all I can picture is a fruit covered in ominously grinning faces.

But something about her voice... settles me. I can sense that she's nervous, but she appears to be a kind enough human and is enthusiastic about our future.

I think this will work in my favor.

CHAPTER THREE

AMARA

ROTH'KAR LISTENS ATTENTIVELY as I tell him all about Halloween and how kids dressed in costumes go from house to house, asking for candy.

"Trick-or-treat?" he asks. "The children are threatening to do something foul to you unless you bestow them some candy?"

I can't help a laugh. "You're right. The idea is kinda messed up. Guess it's a good thing they're just children."

"Their smallness is deceptive," he says in a very serious tone.

I give him an odd look, but I won't be deterred from my enthusiasm about Halloween. "Still, it's a really fun holiday, and I love seeing what costumes everyone is wearing! People also like to put out scary decorations. Like when the kids walk up, a witch screams."

He looks bewildered. "The intention is to frighten?"

"Yes! That's the whole point of Halloween. To get

scared. People even pay to go to haunted houses to get scared out of their minds."

"I cannot imagine such a thing as *intentionally* going to be frightened," he says, shaking his head. "A Karthinian would avoid such a thing. One does not need the additional cortisol."

"Well, you don't have to do it. In Mexico, there's a different holiday called the Day of the Dead, and there are all these cool traditions…"

"Day of the Dead?" Roth'kar is aghast. "So obsessed with death, you humans!"

I clear my throat and decide to move on. "Anyway, Halloween is at the end of October, so… in three weeks. And the parties, oh my god. You've never seen anything like it. My friend Marguerite throws this huge thing with bubbling cauldrons and spooky music, and everybody gets totally toasted. It's so fun."

"Toasted?" He squints, as if thinking. "My translator suggests bread that has been in the oven?"

"Um, like, really drunk. We drink a lot of alcohol." Do Karthinians have alcohol?

A moment passes. "Ah," Roth'kar says suddenly, as if his translator has just given him the answer. "A substance that dulls your nervous system."

"Sure, it's technically a downer, but it amps the fun factor!" I slow down as we approach our exit off the highway. It was a bit of a drive to the spaceport, but I'm lucky I live near one at all. There are only four in the United States. "You get a little loose-limbed after a few drinks, start dancing, maybe make out…"

I cut myself off there with a sigh. Been a long time

since I had a Halloween that ended in making out. But maybe that will change.

Roth'kar cocks his head, his antennae bobbing. "What is this, 'make out'?"

Oh, boy. "Well, it's, uh…" I fumble for the right words. "We'll get to that later. Hopefully. Maybe?" God, what am I saying?

His frown grows deeper as my words confuse him. "I cannot help you with that question unless I know what it is."

I try to keep my eyes on the road as my face heats. "Advanced topic! Let's stick to the basics."

It's another twenty minutes to the apartment, during which time Roth'kar stares out the window. He touches the glass again, like he's trying to reach out beyond it into the trees.

We approach the city limits and wind deeper into town until we've reached my building, where I head down into the parking garage.

Finally, we're ready for Roth'kar to see my place. Rather, *our* place.

I go to unload his bags, but he already has it in his hand.

"That's all you've got?" I ask, rooting around the trunk. Why didn't I notice sooner that he had no belongings? "Just the one bag?"

"It has all I need."

"Huh." So, no wardrobe. Got it. I don't know where I'm going to find more clothes for an alien with four arms, though. He can't very well wear the same odd outfit he's wearing now every day here on Earth. It'll get dirty, and he attracts enough attention with four arms and purple skin.

There are other aliens living here now, of course, ever since the Frahma arrived. A few of them settled, as have other species, but off-worlders are still few and far between. And even fewer are those who have come here through the Matching Program.

Maybe I can order a wardrobe for him online. If I can find a giant unicorn head, which I wore for Fiona's birthday last year, I can find clothes for someone with four arms.

I lead Roth'kar into the elevator, and his eyes get a bit bigger as I press the button for my floor and the doors close. He reaches out to hang on to the railing as the elevator jerks into motion. He mutters something, glancing around us like the elevator might fall apart.

"What's wrong?" I offer what I hope is a tame but friendly smile. He doesn't seem to react well when I give him a bigger one, as if he's being blinded by a bright light, so I'm toning it down.

"This elevator," he says. "Our elevators are much faster. And not quite so… rickety."

That doesn't surprise me. The elevator dings as it stops, and the doors open. "Tell me more about your home planet?" I ask him as we step out.

"Oh. I don't have one."

"What? Where did you come from?" How could he not have a home planet?

"I lived on a spaceship. *New Dro'thar II*. It's where my people relocated once our planet, Dro'thar, became uninhabitable."

I stop as we near my door and stare at him. "What happened to it?"

"Well, we destroyed it."

This catches me off-guard. "How?"

He sighs as I fit my key into my doorknob. "With negligence. Abuse. Mistreatment. Greed." His teeth grind together. "My ancestors were fools."

Roth'kar feels so passionately about this. I want to comfort him and tell him that his new home won't suffer the same fate, but it's hard not to look around us and wonder.

"Well, you have a planet now," I say, pausing to put a hand on his arm. He stares down at where I'm touching him, then lifts his eyes to mine again, but he doesn't shake me off. "And maybe you can help protect this one from the same fate."

His brows rise.

"It has its flaws, but I think Earth is all right. We have blobfish and Taco Tuesdays." I pat him once more and open the front door to show him inside.

"Taco Tuesdays," he echoes. "Is this related to that 'Mexican food' the little Frahma mentioned?"

"Ooh, so it's famous even in space?"

I spent the last three days hurriedly tidying up, making as warm and welcoming of a space for him as I could. I got rid of a lot of junk, which I tend to collect, to make my apartment feel a little more minimalist—like he could add his own details to it.

I want this to be a home for both of us someday, if he's open to it. He seems shy and reserved, but after learning where he comes from, I think I understand. He's probably overwhelmed by Earth, and I need to give him time and space to get settled before I can get to know the true Roth'kar.

"This is it," I say, gesturing at the kitchen off to the right of the entryway, and to the living room up ahead. "Home sweet home."

Roth'kar stands in the doorway, unmoving, as he takes in the apartment. I can't read his expression, which seems to be the norm, as he scans each object.

"This is all yours?" he asks at last, stepping inside so I can close the door behind him. It's a pretty average sized two-bedroom apartment. The kitchen is small, and in the bathroom, the door gets a little too close to the toilet. It's nothing special.

"All *ours*," I correct with a smile. His antennae jump to attention, and I find it curious how they seem to betray things his eyes don't always get across. "Feel free to make changes however you like. I want this to feel like your place, too."

He doesn't speak for a long moment, so I head in to show him where he'll be staying. But his voice stops me.

"Thank you. Thank you for... this."

I don't know what *this* refers to, but I smile anyway. "No problem. Come on in. Let's put your stuff in the bedroom."

He stiffens briefly in the doorway.

"Don't worry, I'll be in the guest room." I gesture to follow me, and I lead him away from the living room and down the hall, where there are three doors—two bedrooms and a bathroom. "You'll be in here." I open the bedroom door, gesturing to my bed. "And I'll be over here."

Looking puzzled, he follows me to the guest room, where the futon has been set up against the wall.

"But this is clearly your personal room," Roth'kar says as he peers into my bedroom. "That's where you usually sleep, yes?"

I give an uncertain bob of my head. "Sure. But you're taller than I am, so you'll be sleeping on the bed. Until, um, we decide on different arrangements."

"Different arrangements." He levels his gaze on me. "I must insist that you sleep in your own bed, Amara. And I will either sleep in it with you or in this other room, whichever makes you more comfortable."

My mouth falls open. "You want to sleep together already?"

He cocks his head. "My translator says there are two meanings to this phrase."

Oh, jeez. We're not even close to that yet.

"In the bed," I clarify. "You want to sleep there with me?"

"I am fine in the other room, as well," he says with measured ease.

I had just assumed we'd sleep in separate places, being as we're, well, strangers. Does he want to just jump right in?

That's an approach, I guess.

"Um, why don't we decide at bedtime?" I feel much too awkward for this conversation already. "I'll make dinner, and we can talk about it."

I head back to the kitchen, and after a beat, Roth'kar follows along behind me. There, I pull out chicken thighs, dried apricots and rice to make a tagine, thinking it might be fun to introduce him to some Moroccan food, where my mother's family comes from. I'm a little Moroccan, a little Greek, with another small portion of Romanian thrown in from my father's father.

Eventually Roth'kar seats himself at the dining room table, remaining quiet as I work cutting the thighs. I need to come up with something for us to talk about, but I'm the sort of person who has a single spicy Bloody Mary and tells you her life story, so it shouldn't be a problem.

"Tell me more about living on a spaceship," I say as I sear the meat. "This will take at least an hour to cook, so we have time."

Roth'kar's resting all four of his hands on the table, which looks like an optical illusion. "There's not much to say. My living quarters were... not this big." He glances around us at my tiny little condo, and he's obviously impressed. What was it like where he comes from? "You have a lovely home, Amara."

It's so sincerely spoken that my face heats. "Oh, well, thank you. I think I've been wanting to share it with someone for a long time. I got this two-bedroom place last year, and I don't know why. A room for my cat, I guess. Not that he used it. He was always trying to follow me into the bathroom."

Roth'kar furrows his brow, waiting for his translator.

"Ah, a cat is a small animal," he says. "You keep small animals in your home? Where is it? I have not seen it."

"He died." My throat closes up just thinking about Elvis. "I'd had him since I was a teenager. I guess it was just his time, but..."

I sniffle, holding the tears at bay.

"Gosh," I say, waving a hand in front of my face. "Sorry. Didn't mean to get all gushy about my cat."

But Roth'kar is studying me intently. "What is that coming out of your eyes?"

I try to think of what he means, then realize a few tears must have slipped free. I wipe one off my cheek. "I cried a little. Humans do it when we're sad."

He blinks. "Fascinating. A physical reaction to your pain." He shakes his head. "I'm sorry. About your 'Elvis.'"

"It's okay. It just made me realize how lonely I am." I turn my attention to chopping the vegetables. "That's why I applied for the Matching Program, I think. There was a hole in my life I was filling with Elvis, until I couldn't any longer."

Roth'kar tilts his head. "You wanted a permanent companion."

That's one way to put it. "Yeah. Someone who will stay with me… for a long time." I brighten. "And someone who can use the toilet and doesn't need me to empty their litter box!"

I think I might have earned a hint of a smile from the stoic alien. I'm rather pleased with myself as I put the food in the oven.

"I don't know of this *litter box,* but I can use a waste unit just fine," he says. "Though you might have to teach me how."

I remember the elevator. "Our *waste units* probably aren't as cool as yours."

Roth'kar shrugs. "I would say ours are a normal temperature."

When I snort, he gives me a quizzical look.

"Okay. Let's go figure out the bathroom while that's cooking. Seems like a good place to start."

CHAPTER FOUR

ROTH'KAR

A FASCINATING CREATURE, this human. Kindness radiates off her, and I enjoy watching the curve of her hip as she works over the counter making dinner. A sliver of guilt wedges itself in my chest at how earnestly she wants a partner.

"I have work tomorrow, but it's Friday, and then we'll be home free," she says.

"And Friday is...?"

"Oh! Right. I forget you don't know Earth things." Her laughter is lively. "Friday is the end of the work week here. So I'll be at my day job tomorrow until five, but then I'm off that night and the next two days. And we can do all kinds of stuff!"

Coming into this, I expected she would have work of some sort to pay for our living expenses. I had thought perhaps she'd be a farmer and I could help out in that way, but I'm not sure what her job entails.

"What do you do? For your work?"

She seems instantly repelled by my question, wrinkling up her nose. "I'm a paper pusher."

"Paper pusher?" I repeat. "What benefit do you get from pushing paper around?"

"Just means that my job feels pointless." She sighs in a way that's distinctly bored. "It's fine. I like the hours and the benefits, and I don't work too hard. But it gets old."

Perhaps I understand even better now. She is seeking satisfaction in her life and isn't receiving it in her place of work.

"Drudgery," I say. My own work, when I could get it, was often drudgery. Sometimes I cleaned out old pipes, or hauled scrap from one place to another, or got paid to pick through said scrap. I always walked away from those jobs with shredded hands.

She nods. "Yes, drudgery. It's the same thing every day. I wouldn't mind it if, you know, it felt worthwhile. Paying for this apartment." She gestures around us. "Making dinner, stuff like that. I thought it would be better if there was someone waiting for me at home."

She bashfully turns her head at this, taking a nervous sip of her water. I realize she means me, and so I sit up and extend one of my upper hands to her.

Curious, Amara extends her own hand, and I clasp it in mine, twining our fingers together. Her tan complexion darkens.

"I would be happy to be here when you arrive home tomorrow," I say. "What should I do while you're gone? I can cook, as well."

"You should get settled! Explore, maybe. Get to know the neighborhood a little." She taps her chin. "Shoot, I forgot to get an extra key made. I'll leave it with you tomorrow, and you'll just have to promise not to lock us out."

My translator hurriedly provides an image of a "key" turning in a lock, and I understand. Far more basic than a scan card. Very rustic.

We talk some more about what activities her neighborhood offers—there's a convenience store, which I understand sells small necessities and snacks, a restaurant, and another place that I still don't quite grasp what it does.

"Paycheck advances," she says. "Predatory. They give you a loan on your future paycheck. A scam, if you ask me, that takes advantage of poor people."

Her righteous fury surprises me. She seems quite well-off, if the large accommodations are any indication, so what interest does she have in the plight of the poor? She is an interesting woman.

Not long after, the food is ready. She serves a cooked grain that comes out yellow, which she explains is saffron rice, then meat and vegetables from the "tagine" dish.

The food is a revelation. I've never tasted anything with so much *character*, so much spice and intensity. Each bite is an explosion of flavor, and I find myself absolutely, deliriously ravenous for it. I spoon every last bit from my plate into my mouth, and then look up to find Amara staring at me.

"Do you like it?" she asks, a smile teasing at her lips. "There's more."

I give her a hasty nod before helping myself to another portion, which I consume just as quickly, using another one of the utensils—the *fork*—so that I can eat with three hands at the same time while I hold the plate in my fourth.

Finally, I'm finished, and I can't eat another bite. But oh, how badly I want to. It was the most delicious meal I've ever had in my life.

"Wow, you can really pack it away," Amara says playfully as she gathers up my plate. I want to assist her in cleaning up, but I can barely move. "Stay there. I'll take care of it. Then we should get settled."

Ah, I know what she refers to: my inopportune suggestion about sleeping in the same bed, which clearly took her aback. But I don't want to make her sleep on that rather small cot in the other room and kick her out of her own living quarters.

"I guess sleeping in the same bed is expected of a husband and wife," she goes on, her back facing me as she washes the dishes, then loads them into a machine. "Do you, um, feel comfortable with that? Really?"

It's less a matter of comfort and more of doing what I think will please her. I want these thirty days to end with Amara deciding to keep me so I can get my residency on Earth.

"If you are not ready, then I'll sleep in the adjoining room," I assure her. "The other bed doesn't bother me."

She pauses, back still turned. Then she slides the plate into the rack and closes the machine with a *click*. When she looks at me, her lips are pursed with uncertainty. It's fascinating how much humans get across with their facial expressions.

"I just don't know you that well yet," she says, wringing her hands. "But I do think you are, erm—" She coughs. "Attractive? I mean, I would like to get to that point. Of sleeping together. In the bed. In the future, when we know each other better?"

This is good. She is clearly not at the point of discussing intercourse yet, but she does have an interest in sharing intimate space.

"Then we will wait until the time is right." I rise from my chair, finally able to move my body again after how much I ate. "I will sleep in the other room for now."

"But it's so small—"

I put my lower arms on my hips and cross the upper pair across my chest. "I will be fine. You have a lovely home, with every creature comfort." The waste receptacle seemed outdated at best, but at least it was far cleaner than the one I shared with five other adults in the Hole. "I will not be wanting for anything."

She considers this, then lets out a resigned sigh.

"All right." She offers me a smile. "You're a nice guy, Roth'kar."

The compliment is so sincere that I'm surprised by it. She takes a step closer to me and holds out her hand.

"I feel like we didn't really meet properly at the space-port." Her ring glints on her second-to-last finger. The symbol of our "marriage." "But I'm really glad that you decided to do this with me."

I try to smile my best in return and take her hand in mine. She squeezes it, then withdraws.

"Whenever you're up for a hug, though, let me know." A mischievous expression crosses her face. "I like hugging."

I consider wrapping my four arms around her right then and there to cement the bond between us, but I am getting the sense that Amara needs more courting. It is very different from my past experiences with females. I will have to tread carefully.

"Then we shall hug at an agreed-upon date," I suggest.

"Oh. Okay." Amara gives me a shy smile. "Let's set up a time."

I press my hands to my chest, then tilt my head up. "Goodnight."

She waves her hand awkwardly. "Goodnight, then." As I turn around and head to my room, though, she calls over my shoulder. "Do you need a toothbrush or anything?"

The words make sense taken in parts—a brush for one's teeth—but it's a barbaric way to clean the incisors.

I hold up my bag. "I have a cleaning unit."

"A cleaning... unit?" She cocks her head, so I retrieve it. The unit is inside a container, which I open and then pull the curved cleaner out. I place it in my mouth, around my teeth, and it vibrates for only a few moments. Then I switch it to the lower set, press it again, and I'm finished. I take the unit into her "bathroom" and clean it out in the sink, which she showed me how to operate earlier.

Amara's mouth is agape when I return. "Wow. Totally jealous." She straightens. "All right, then. Tomorrow at work, I'll shop online for some new clothes for you so you're not always wearing the same thing."

I give a brief nod of appreciation. I suppose I do need something else to wear on this planet, as unlike Karthinians—who all wear mostly the same clothes—it appears humans all dress differently, in a vast array of colors.

"Thank you," I finally answer. My antennae quiver with pleasure, because it will be nice to wear something besides the uniform I've had for years. Amara's own clothes are unusual in fashion but clean and new, and I wonder if I might match her.

"No problem. We'll get you a whole new wardrobe. Maybe people won't even notice you're blue!" She snickers. "Though the antennae will probably give you away."

With that, we each retreat to our respective rooms. The bed Amara called a "futon" is made up prettily, with a soft pillow and many equally soft blankets. I've never had anything but my scratchy sleep bag, and the sensation of the plush fabric on my skin is lovely. Although my heels hang off the edge, the cushioning under my back is more than sufficient.

I should go to sleep and be prepared for what tomorrow brings, but I stay awake for some time remembering how just two days ago, I was preparing for this journey in my room in the Hole, saying goodbye to Shar'sak and Zono, who slept in the rooms adjoining mine in our cubicle. Now I am peering through the slatted coverings over the window, where outside I can distinguish the edges of trees, past a bright light over the street.

This is a backward place in many ways, but the future feels open and inviting. I've made it off *New Dro'thar II*: the place where I was born, where my father died in an engine fire and my mother died of fever, where all the friends I've left behind remain. I wish I could have brought them along, but they encouraged me on this journey, wanting the best for me.

For them, I will make the best life I can here, and Amara will help me achieve that.

CHAPTER FIVE

AMARA

I REGRET NOT TAKING the day off work after bringing Roth'kar home. It was an oversight on my part, but to be fair, Roth'kar's arrival had been somewhat of a surprise and I hadn't been thinking clearly.

He's still in his room when I wake up to the sound of my alarm and get ready for work. Perhaps he's sleeping off his long trip. I decide not to wake him before I scurry out.

My work bestie, Kendall, is the first one to ask me about my new alien husband. She's the only one in the office who knows that I applied for the Matching Program, and of course, I told her when I was approved. I stir the creamer into my coffee, keeping my voice low.

"He has antennae," I tell her. "Little antennae on his head. And... they're freakishly cute."

Her brows rise. "Antennae? Huh."

"Oh. And four arms."

This time, her eyes bug out of her head. "What? Four arms? Four hands? How many fingers?"

"Five, thank goodness. I mean, I'd obviously still welcome him if he had four or seven or whatever! But it's nice that's familiar when the rest of him is all purply blue."

Kendall shakes her head in disbelief. "Wild. Amara, hooked up with a purple, four-armed alien. I love this for you."

I laugh as we make our way back to our desks. "Yeah, but I have to figure out a clothing situation for him."

"I've got someone." We sit down next to each other in front of our computers, on our matching exercise balls. "You know how short I am. She hems all my pants."

I grimace at the thought of needing a bunch of custom-made clothes for Roth'kar. That would add up, fast. But I also knew upon applying what was expected. I agreed to provide everything my new husband needed, and clothes were on that list. I just didn't expect he would have four arms requiring accommodation.

I do my morning work in an hour, then get online to browse for clothes. There are other Karthinians on Earth —look at me, knowing how to say it properly—but the pictures I find are all of handmade goods. It's $150 for a single shirt that would fit his arms.

Oh boy.

On my lunch break, I place a call to the tailor Kendall suggested.

"He has four arms," I repeat when the older woman on the other end doesn't know what to make of my request. "He's an alien. My husband. I need a bunch of clothes for him."

The tailor is quiet for a moment, then she answers, "I can provide a bulk discount. Bring him into the shop tomorrow." Then she hangs up.

Well, that works for me, I guess. A bulk discount sounds appealing.

I'm nervous all day, though, wondering what Roth'kar is up to alone at home. I probably shouldn't have told him to go explore. He doesn't know how traffic signals or pedestrian crossings work. He doesn't have money and he doesn't have a map. He doesn't even have a cell phone so he can call me if something goes wrong.

Man, I'm an idiot. I hope Roth'kar isn't a pancake when I get home.

Since I can't very well run to my condo in the middle of the day and I don't have a landline, I use my anxiety to go internet shopping for things we're going to need. First thing I do is buy him a phone, then a nice waterproof case to go with it. On my way home, I'll make a copy of the house key and pull out some cash to give to Roth'kar should he go wandering about.

I left him food in the fridge but neglected to show him how to use the microwave. God, I'm bad at this alien wife thing.

After lunch, I get some more work done, just enough to get my urgent tasks off my plate. The rest can wait until next week. Then I make up an excuse to my boss about not feeling well and leave the office early.

I drive home as fast as I can and roar into the parking garage with a squeal of my tires. When I get back to the condo, the door is unlocked, which I hope means that my new husband is at home and safe. But inside, the lights are off, and I can't see anyone.

Fuck.

"Hello?" I call out. "Roth'kar?"

There's no answer. I flip on the lights and peer into my room, then his room, both of which are dark.

Damn. The afternoon is fading fast. He must have gone somewhere, and I gave him no tools whatsoever with which to survive.

Then I hear a yawn, and spin around to find four hands rising into the air above the couch. Roth'kar sits up, then yawns again, covering his mouth.

"You're back," he says, getting to his feet abruptly.

"So I am." I let out a relieved breath. "I'm glad you're here."

He simply nods. "I tried to exit the building as you suggested, but when I followed the signs for *exit*, a very loud alarm went off. I was escorted back to your apartment by a rather large man in a blue uniform."

I knew it would all go wrong, but at least he didn't get any farther than the fire exit.

"I'm so sorry." I fall into one of the chairs at the table. "I should have at least shown you around before suggesting you go out."

Roth'kar sits across from me and reaches out to put a gentle hand on my arm. "It's no cause for concern. I explained the situation, and the uniformed man led me back here."

I shake my head. I can't believe he's had a run-in with the cops already, and I haven't even had time to explain that he should avoid them.

Roth'kar continues. "He said, however, I need some sort of *vee-sa*?"

I squint. "Vee-sa? Oh! A visa!" I didn't even think

about that. All aliens that settle on Earth need a galactic visa, and one of my first priorities should have been to take him to the registration office.

That will probably take all day. At least we won't have to go to the DMV, though.

"Wow. Good thing that cop was understanding," I say with a sigh. That could've gone badly very quickly for Roth'kar. Now I feel even worse. "Did the matching agency give you a temporary visa?"

Roth'kar stares at me. "I do not know what this vee-sa is."

"It's, like, a really stupid permit you need to have to be on Earth. I can't believe Gazargo didn't give you one."

Roth'kar tilts his head, then spins on his heel, zooming down the hallway to his room. He returns with his bag, which he opens, revealing pitifully few contents before he produces a folder.

"Is this the *vee-sa*?"

I open the folder to find exactly what I'm looking for, right on top. I exhale with relief.

"Good, it's here. Keep it on you, then I can at least take you to the tailor."

Rothkar's antennae bob when he cocks his head. "Tailor?"

"A tailor measures you and then makes clothes, or alters clothes, to fit." I hold out my arms. "Since humans only have two of these, there's not much in the way of Earth-made outfits that will work for you."

He nods in understanding. "Thank you, Amara. For doing this for me."

I wave him off. "It's my job as your wife to take care of you." It's strange how this word feels slipping off my tongue. *Wife.* "I wanted you to come here and share my life with me."

Those glowing blue eyes study me, different enough from a human's that I'm acutely aware of our differences. When I opted to marry an alien, I didn't consider just how *alien* he would be.

"Then, as your 'husband,' what is my job?"

"Your job?" I stare blankly at him, because I have no idea how to answer. I didn't consider too deeply what my future husband might want to contribute to our relationship. "I... I don't know. I mean, you don't have to have a job. I make enough money to support us."

Roth'kar is quiet, still watching me, as if puzzling over me. I feel a little bare under his gaze.

"I suppose I will have to find a job, then," he says at last. "Something I can do to help you and make your life easier."

It's sweet that he wants to contribute something.

"Well, do you know how to cook?" I ask, as I sidle into the kitchen to get started on dinner.

"I cook." He follows me, gazing curiously around the kitchen. "I can't say that I know how to use any of these devices, though. Or how to make human food."

I brighten. "At least you know how! That's what's important." I pull out a pan, then fish through the fridge for ingredients. I had a few meals planned, but seeing as how much Roth'kar eats, I may have to go shopping again soon. "I can show you."

"I would appreciate that."

Roth'kar is a good student as I demonstrate dicing vegetables, then hand over the knife so he can mimic it. I

"No, not every night. Actually, very few nights." My lips screw up at the thought of just how much fast food I've eaten lately, ever since Elvis died. "I eat out a lot."

"Eat out?"

"At a restaurant. Somewhere you go where people prepare the food for you, and you just eat it."

His brow furrows. "Like our slophouse."

I'm not sure I heard him right. "Slophouse?"

"Where we ate when we didn't eat at home." He thinks for a moment. "The translator says it is somewhat like a cafeteria."

"No restaurants? Like, places where you can choose what to eat?"

"Choose?" He shakes his head. "The food comes out, it goes on your tray, and you eat it. Seconds cost extra chips. If you don't eat it all, you can put it in your shirt, but then it tastes like shirt. Sometimes shirt is an improvement, though." He nods at the chicken in my hands. "Will you show me how to cut this up so I can do it in the future?"

It's adorable how much he wants to learn, so I stand a little closer as we start the lesson.

42

CHAPTER SIX

ROTH'KAR

I SHOULD LIKELY NOT TALK TOO much about the Hole, about life on *New Dro'thar II*. I do not want or need Amara pitying me, and I also fear it might become too obvious why I came to Earth. I don't think my plan would be received well.

Instead, I divert Amara's attention to showing me how to cook in her home, using the "stove," the "oven"—both of which appear to be the same device—and the toaster— which is yet another "oven" but smaller—for quickly melting cheese.

The cheese is, I must admit, my favorite part. It's gooey and salty and absolutely perfect. I think, after our meal, that I could eat much more cheese.

"Earth has such a wide variety of flavors," I say thoughtfully as I pack away my second portion. Amara is smiling the whole time, like my ravenous hunger for the food she made has pleased her.

"Oh, this is only a fraction of it," she says, clapping her hands. "There's so much more to show you. Indian food, Japanese food, Mexican food…" Her eyes fall closed, like she's dreaming of this cuisine. "Food from all over the world tastes different."

"And you can get all that here?" I ask. "You don't have to go to another place to eat their food?"

Amara laughs. "Yes, we can get it here. It might not be authentic, but it's good enough." She taps her chin. "I wonder if you'd like sushi."

"Soo-shi?"

"Raw fish with rice and seaweed. And other stuff, too."

My translator supplies an image for a sea-faring animal, and I wrinkle my nose at the idea of eating it raw. Everything you eat in the Hole is cooked to eliminate disease.

"It's good, I promise," Amara says, registering my expression with amusement. "I'll only take you to eat yummy food."

After the two meals she's made for me, I believe this is true.

That night, I wonder if Amara will invite me into her bed. It is my duty, after all, to make sure she is content in all ways. And I wouldn't terribly mind it, either—she is appealing and attractive with her wide hips and long-lashed eyes.

But after dinner, when we've sat and talked for some time about different regions of Earth and the kinds of foods they have there, Amara bids me goodnight and goes to her bedroom, leaving me in the hallway alone.

I furrow my brow. I spent much of today looking up with the communicator what information I could about human anatomy, and I believe I've memorized all her potential erogenous zones. But she doesn't seem interested, which worries me.

What if she sends me back because she doesn't find me attractive? What if, by the end of the trial, she doesn't want to complete the ritual, and I don't get my citizenship?

I slink back to the futon and make myself comfortable, trying not to dread what may or may not happen in the future. This was only our first day. I still have time to prove to her I can be a good husband.

I'll be the best husband. I'll learn the oven *and* the stove, and make everything with cheese on it, and Amara will keep me until the deal is done. Then I can decide what's next.

I awaken to sun coming in my window, and I blink hard at the brightness of it. The sun isn't like other kinds of light —it's brighter than any kind of artificial light we had on *New Dro'thar II*, but in a gentle way. There's a different quality to it that's... magical. Life-giving. I rise out of bed and lift my head to the window, resting my cheek against it to savor the warmth.

That's why I attempted to go outside yesterday. I wanted simply to stand in the fresh air and breathe it in. I hope I'll get a chance today when we go to this *tailor*. I want to feel the sun directly on my skin, to soak it up and revel in it.

After putting on my shabby clothes and cinching my

belt, I find Amara waiting by the door with a big smile on her face. I am beginning to appreciate her smiles, how they warm up her whole face. It is welcoming and genuine.

She offers me her arm, and I'm not sure what she wants me to do with it. With a giggle, she loops her hand around my elbow. The touch is so intimate, so companionable, that I stiffen.

"Are you worried about falling?" I ask her, holding her tighter just in case.

"No, no, not at all." Amara gently squeezes. "I just thought it might be... nice."

I try to relax. I am her husband, after all, and this must be a common behavior between husbands and wives on Earth.

After showing me the correct way to leave the building —*not* the same direction as the exit sign, which makes no sense to me—we're out on the street. Other humans pass by, many of them staring as they go. I pause there and close my eyes, lifting my head to feel the warm sun on my face.

"Do you like it?" Amara asks, and I open my eyes again. "You said you grew up on a spaceship. Was there a sun close by?"

I shake my head. "I've always lived with artificial light. We have ultraviolet, of course, in order to survive. But never real sunshine."

"We should go for a walk in the park!" She leads me by the arm down the paved pathway that runs alongside the asphalt street. "If you've never seen trees up close before, I bet you would like it."

This is an exciting idea. I could get close to the trees,

perhaps even touch them. I want to know more about these big, leafy plants.

"Oh, yes. I would enjoy this."

Amara comes to an abrupt stop at the edge of the sidewalk, but I try to continue.

"We have to wait," she says, keeping me from going any farther. "See that light?" She raises her hand and points at a lit symbol across the street. "That means stop. After a while, it changes into a little green man, and then you can go."

"Green man?"

Cars pass by quickly, and I think how silly it is they still have ground vehicles when they can prove so hazardous to pedestrians. On *New Dro'thar II,* all vehicles travel on a separate raised level, while pedestrians remain on the floor so there is never any risk of being hit.

I have learned yet another rule of this world. Don't get hit by a car. Wait for the green man.

"The traffic lights are the same way," Amara says as we wait. "Red means stop, green means it's safe to go."

"And yellow?" I ask, pointing at one of the lights as it changes.

"Um... it's like, stop if you can, but don't slam on your brakes. Unless someone's right behind you, then I usually go through it. But you have to kiss your hand and slap the roof so the cops don't pull you over."

Driving sounds complicated. Her world is dangerous.

Then the red hand vanishes, replaced by a green walking figure.

"So we can walk now?" I ask, and Amara beams.

"You've got it."

As we go, Amara and I cover many more essential

subjects, such as walking on the right side of the sidewalk, when a small, four-legged creature steps out in front of me.

I've never seen anything like it, and I nearly jump out of my skin.

"What is that?" I ask Amara in a hoarse voice. The furry animal is, thank goodness, held back by a restraint, but the moment it sees me it lets out a terrible, sharp sound that blasts my eardrums.

I leap back, startled, right into a bush.

"Sorry," says the woman trying to keep a hold on the animal. "He's never seen an alien before."

I find I'm holding onto Amara's arm rather tightly as we leave it behind, me leading us at a quick clip down the street.

"It's okay," Amara says, patting me. "That was just a dog. Have you never seen a pet before?"

"Never."

Most of our food is arthropod protein, from insects raised in containers on higher levels of the ship. We certainly do not have animals as *pets*. You could keep a cricket in a box, I suppose, but one of your friends would probably sneak it as a snack.

"Well, dogs are mostly harmless. You shouldn't pet one without asking first, though. I never pet dogs I see on the street just to be safe."

"Just to be safe?" I glance back at the animal warily. It raises one leg and urinates on a tree. "Safe from what?"

"Dogs can bite. I mean, most animals do, but they usually won't bother you unless you bother them."

"Earth animals... bite?" This is a disturbing thought. Especially when one is simply out and about on a leash.

"Not all of them. A bird could peck you. Which probably hurts, but not that bad?" Amara contemplates this. "I think it would hurt if they pecked you in the eye, like in that one movie."

"Pecked you in the *eye*?" I don't know what this *bird* is, but I don't like it already. "How would it accomplish that?"

"Birds fly!" Amara points up at the sky. "They're winged animals. Like planes."

I stare at her. "Birds are like..." My translator supplies me with a massive flying vehicle, large enough to swallow ten humans. "Planes?"

Horrifying. And they're just flying around?

Amara waves her hands wildly. "No, no, I just meant that birds fly the same way planes do. Birds are small." She pauses thoughtfully. "Usually. Though I do hear condors are big."

I'm frozen, imagining the plane-sized bird pecking my eyes out. Maybe I made a mistake by coming to Earth. How has such a soft woman survived here for so long? I'm aghast the rest of the way to the tailor's, second-guessing our decision to visit the park later.

Inside the building it's rather dark, with moody lighting above racks of clothes. A woman with deep wrinkles and gray hair slides out from behind a counter to greet us.

"Ah, the alien," she says, taking in the sight of me. She strums her chin. "Four arms. How interesting." She beckons us to follow and heads into the back of the store. Amara takes my hand and leads me after her. There are two partitions with curtains, and the woman whips out a long string and sits on a stool uncomfortably close to me.

She inspects my arms closely, and I shoot Amara a confused look.

"She's measuring you. For your new clothes."

I stand still as the tailor holds up her tape and measures the space between my upper armpit and my lower shoulder before making some notes. Then she measures around my chest, my neck, and waist, noting all of it.

"The bad news," the woman says, rising, "is that I'll have to make all his shirts by hand. I thought I could simply add additional sleeves, but given his anatomy, he'll need new garments made to fit him."

I can tell this is not what Amara wanted to hear. Her face visibly wilts, and I curse that I couldn't have at least come with some Earth-appropriate clothing. She probably didn't expect she'd have to pay such a high bill to have me around.

"All right," she finally says. "You said you could give me a bulk discount?"

"How many garments do you need?"

She glances at me. "I can do the laundry every week, so... what about seven shirts? And a jacket for the cold weather."

The tailor whips a little pad of paper out of her pocket, scribbles something on it, rips it off and hands it to Amara. Her dark complexion pales.

"Really?" She grinds her teeth together. "All right."

Whatever number is written on that paper must be upsetting. I want to argue that I would be fine with far fewer items of clothing, but before I can even open my mouth, Amara gives me a stern look.

"You need clothes. Don't even start, antennae boy."

I press my lips together to keep the words from coming out, because I don't want to upset her even further.

Amara squints as she runs a rectangular card through a machine at the front counter, and I believe it is some sort of credit system. Credit is given to Karthinians higher up the food chain, those who live above the Hole and can be trusted to pay back the money they spend. Amara must be well-off in Earth society to have access to credit.

"Thank you," Amara says to the tailor, her expression pinched.

"No problem. I'll have the clothes ready for you next week." The old woman stops me before we can depart. "I forgot to ask. Do you have color preferences?"

I stare blankly. Colors? My uniform has always been this same off-white, and I've never worn anything else.

"I think a dark blue would look good," the tailor says thoughtfully. "Maybe some grays."

"I…" I glance at Amara, who is wearing a purple shirt with blue jeans. I like how it looks on her, setting off her brown skin and dark hair. "I like purple," I announce after a moment.

The tailor cocks her head, then, after some contemplation, takes more notes before waving us off. Amara takes my arm in her hand, and we depart the shop together.

She has already done so much for me. I need to learn how to cook Earth meals properly to pay her back.

As we head home, we pass the dog and its owner coming down the street, and I move between it and Amara in case it decides to bite.

Perhaps there is something I can do for her—keep her safe in this strange and dangerous world.

CHAPTER SEVEN

AMARA

IT WAS obvious by the drooping of his antennae that Roth'kar didn't know what to do with the tailor's question. *Do you have any color preferences?* I remembered his empty bag and how he came to me with nothing but the clothes he was wearing.

It was as if the question made no sense.

There are so many things I want to know about him, but Roth'kar isn't the most forthcoming about himself. Maybe I just need to get him in the right environment and he'll open up a little.

I want to get to know my new husband better.

It's more than a few blocks to the park, but eventually we make it. There's a sand pit where some little kids are playing, and a jungle gym next to it. I loop my hand around Roth'kar's arm again, and this time, he gently lays his hand on top of mine.

"I like this walking," he says. He isn't looking at me,

but his cheeks are a tinge darker purple.

This brings a smile to my face. He enjoys me holding his arm, I think. That's a good step.

The children on the playground catch his attention, and Roth'kar flinches when one of them screams.

"Are they injured?" He looks prepared to leap into action should one of the children be hurt, but I hold him back, trying not to laugh.

"It's okay. They're fine. That's just how children play."

"*Human* children," he says, still giving the playground a wary look, as if he might need to catch a falling Earthling at any moment. "I have never seen a Karthinian child behave that way."

I wonder what growing up on his spaceship was like if this is how he feels about kids playing.

"Did you ever run around and play with your friends?"

Roth'kar's antennae curl down, though his expression betrays nothing.

"I did not." He turns toward the trees ahead. "Do they have names, these different sorts of trees?"

So he wants to change the subject. What was his childhood like that he avoids talking about it? Guess I'm going to play amateur arborist.

I tip my head and study the branches overhead. "I don't know all the names, but I can tell you that there are two kinds."

I explain the difference between deciduous and coniferous trees, and he pulls off a leaf. He rubs it as we walk, absorbing the texture of it.

"Marvelous," Roth'kar says after I've been quiet for a while. "There is so much life here. So many varieties."

Then, out in front of us, a squirrel shoots across the

path. Roth'kar leaps back, nearly pulling me down to the ground, and he lets out a sharp cry.

"What is it?!" I search for the source of his alarm.

The squirrel sprints up the tree, and he points at it. "That... that *thing!*" He clutches his chest like he's trying to stop his heart from escaping. "What was that?"

"A squirrel?" I peer up at it as it scurries away into the tree. "It can't hurt you."

"It can bite," Roth'kar points out. "Like you said. And what if it came back with others? What if you were swarmed by them?" He shivers. "It moves so quick, it would be over before it even started."

I stand there, gaping at the direction his imagination has taken.

"I promise the squirrel won't return with his friends." I take his arm once more and urge him to follow me down the path.

"You don't know that."

Roth'kar's grip is a little more forceful now as we continue. Joggers and cyclists stare as they pass us, but he seems unaffected. Aliens still aren't common on Earth, and a little girl points and shouts, "Mom! Alien!" as she goes by.

"Sorry about that," I say. "You're just... a little alien to them."

"I expected as much when I chose to come here." His lips twitch in the ghost of a smile. "Do not worry about me."

"They're just jealous they don't have four arms, too."

We enjoy the weather together as we walk in a companionable silence. The loop takes us around and back to the start, where we emerge from the trees into the sunshine again. Roth'kar pauses here and gazes up at the sky, his face surprisingly peaceful.

He is beautiful, I must admit, as the light reflects off the surface of his purple-blue skin. His smile returns when he notices me watching him, and Roth'kar offers me his arm to walk home.

It's Saturday night, which usually means a night out with the girls. Fiona shoots me a text as we're on our way back from the park.

"Are you going to bring him out to meet us?" she asks. "Your new alien husband? Or are you going to keep him a secret?"

I finally had to confess the truth when I went to go pick Roth'kar up at the spaceport. Now that my friends know, I should have guessed they would swoop in like vultures, wanting a piece of him.

They're wonderful like that.

"What do you think of meeting my friends tonight?" I ask my new alien husband. His antennae jump to alert.

"Your friends? Of course, I would be pleased to meet them."

He's so agreeable. As long as whatever I'm asking him to agree with doesn't have four legs and a tail.

"All right. We're going to a club, so there will be a lot of sensory input, but—"

Roth'kar gently touches my arm. "Amara, you don't need to protect me. I will tell you if we encounter anything I can't handle."

"Deal?" I ask, holding out my hand.

He blinks at me. "What is your offer?"

I laugh. "The deal is that I won't worry about you, if you promise to tell me if you need to leave."

Roth'kar takes my hand, and we shake.

"You humans do like your hand shaking," he says, stretching his fingers after I've let him go.

I wish I had something to put him in besides his dirty, very obviously alien clothes.

"Can I wash this for you real quick?" I ask. "I know you don't have anything else to wear, but I could get you a towel. It'll take an hour to wash and dry them."

Roth'kar's eyebrows rise. "A towel is not necessary. You are my wife, are you not? Would my nudity offend you?"

I stare at him blankly. He's offering to walk around naked while I wash his clothes?

"Oh, um." I don't even know what to say. Part of me is instantly thrilled. What does he look like under there? I could finally find out if he has two dongs or just one.

Or something else entirely. I didn't consider that. All they told me is that we were "sexually compatible," whatever a Frahma might think that means. God, what if they're totally wrong?

Roth'kar doesn't miss the expression that crosses my face. "I get the sense this might make you uncomfortable."

I rub my hands together. What should I even say? He's right that we're husband and wife now. We'll be seeing a lot of each other naked, and hopefully, doing other things that involve no clothes. That's an essential if we're going to make it in the long term.

But what if what I see is too strange? Too *alien*?

"Maybe we should kiss first," I joke. "Then I can see you bare-assed."

He furrows his brow. "Kiss? The translator is giving me an image that cannot be right."

"What's it saying?"

"That you put one mouth on another mouth?" He sticks out his tongue in disgust. "Such an action can't be hygienic."

I'm strangely disappointed. Maybe he's right—maybe kissing is gross. Of course I wouldn't think so, seeing as it's a part of my own culture. But to an outsider...

"Oh." I swallow hard. "We don't have to do it, then. It was just a joke, anyway."

Roth'kar studies me, not speaking for a long moment, and I fidget under his penetrating, ethereal gaze.

"This disappoints you." It's not a question.

I shrug and force a smile onto my face. "It doesn't!" I lie. "I knew we'd have some differences when you came here. I'm sure there are things in your culture I'd find strange, like if you, um..." I trail off, thinking of our conversation about birds earlier, "...you know, wear feathers and dance around naked to find a wife."

Roth'kar squints at me. "We do not wear feathers and dance around naked. Is this a human custom?"

"No, no! It's just..." I sigh. "Never mind. Why don't you get those clothes off so I can wash them?"

Roth'kar retreats into the bathroom, then emerges a few moments later with a towel wrapped around him. His chest is exposed with the towel circling only around his shapely hips, and I'm... entranced. He has sizable, sculpted pectorals that lead down to a strong abdomen, and his musculature, while different with his four arms, is definitely not unappealing.

Damn. He's fine.

Quickly, I sweep up the clothes and carry them off to the washing machine. Roth'kar waits while I cook us dinner, because I want to have plenty of food inside both of us before we head out on the town.

When the buzzer goes off, I switch the clothes to the dryer, and Roth'kar and I get to eating. But something about our kissing conversation has quieted both of us.

I had a wonderful day today with Roth'kar. I like him. I like him, and I worry it won't work out because we're too different, but by then I'll be attached to him. We've had a good time together so far, but what if he decides I'm not the right fit? What if he chooses to go home and I'm all alone again?

I'm going to show him a good time tonight, I decide. I'll give him a reason to stay.

CHAPTER EIGHT

ROTH'KAR

ALL THROUGHOUT DINNER, although the food is delicious, I am thinking about this *kissing*. It clearly hurt Amara's feelings when I, rather tastelessly, aired my opinion about it.

Maybe I should try kissing before I'm too harsh on Earth customs. They mean a lot to my new wife, clearly, and I don't want to offend her. But it did seem to be a rather unusual act to mash your faces together that way.

I sit in the towel for another half hour until my clothes are dry. Then I change into them, and I'm pleased to find them almost a different color than before—much closer to white. They still do not match Amara's style of dress, but at least I will be fully covered, and we can "go out on the town," as she put it. It did seem to me to be more of a large city, though.

Before we go, Amara retreats to the bathroom for the better part of an hour. Sitting on the couch, I pick up a few booklets she has scattered there, and my translator helps me read them. *Ten ways to drive your man crazy.*

I thought that was a bad thing. Perhaps I am not crazy enough for Amara.

When she emerges sometime later... I almost trip over myself getting to my feet. It's less that she is wearing the little black garment, and more like it has been painted over her. The shape of her breasts is fully visible, and they are heavy and pert. The curve of her hips and thighs couldn't be clearer unless she was naked. Her eyes are much darker, with thick makeup around her lashes that makes her look almost dangerous. Her hair is hanging down in loose, shiny waves.

I can't speak for a long moment. This creature with shining eyes and long, colored nails on her slim fingers is intended to be mine? I'm getting warm in the chest, my heart beating faster as she gets closer.

"What do you think?" Amara asks shyly, flicking some long hair over her shoulder. I track it with my eyes, and that warmth spreads downward, into my abdomen and the base of my culans. The soft ridges awaken, fluttering as blood travels into them.

Oh, no, I need to stop that from happening. If Amara was uncomfortable with the idea of my nudity, she's certainly not prepared for this.

"You look wonderful," I say quickly, adjusting so my erection might look less obvious. "My apologies. You were in the bathroom for a while and I need to..." I clear my throat.

She ushers me on. "Sorry! Go, go!"

I shut the door behind me the second I'm inside, taking a few calming breaths. I did not anticipate my culans would become aroused on their own. Usually if I need to call on them, they must be stroked, coaxed out. But when I unclasp my belt and pull down my leggings, the two culans are clasped tightly together, already shivering. As I lower my hand to them, they part, each one lined with the soft, fleshy ridges that clasp together to unite. They only separate like this when eager to mate, seeking out touch, looking for parts to stimulate.

I pull out my communicator and bring up the screen I had been looking at last night—the diagram of the human female's body. I zoom in on the crotch, where I once again survey the shape of the vagina. It is very different from a Karthinian's culansa, a channel with two paths leading off from it, one to each uterus. No, the vagina has a single entry hole leading to one uterus, and as if imagining it, my culans snap closed again and squeeze together into a single appendage that would, hopefully, fit there. I wrap my hand around it and stroke, gasping when I secrete fluid from between the culans, coating their shivering spines.

I wonder if she'd like how they would feel inside her. They are designed to stimulate as they flutter. Is she as sensitive along her vagina as a Karthinian is?

More of my cum oozes out the sides as I stroke again, and again, hoping I can squeeze out a finish quickly and exit the bathroom before it becomes suspicious. Pumping hard a few more times, my eyes roll back in my head, and my culans seize, their spines shaking wildly as I meet my pinnacle.

I gush all over the floor, which is easy to clean. Then I make a show of flushing the toilet and running the water before stepping back out. Amara is wearing a pair of shoes with high heels on, while a bag on a gold chain hangs from her opposite shoulder. The gold matches her earrings, which glint in the light.

"You ready?" she asks, her lashes falling low over her eyes. They are pure suggestion, oozing sex, and I'm stunned by how my body once again reacts to it.

"I-I believe so."

Amara hooks her hand in my arm, the same way she did on our walk. "Then let's get out of here."

Rather than going in her vehicle, she leads me down the street to a plastic overhang with a big sign reading "59" over the top.

"We're taking the bus!" Amara announces. "That way, I don't have to drive us home later when I'm inevitably wasted."

"Why would anyone waste you?"

She snorts. "It means drinking a lot. So much you can't see straight."

I grimace. "That sounds awful."

"Sounds *fun*, you mean!" She's simply lit up all over, her excitement radiating off her in waves. I find myself soaking it up, curious about what she has planned for us tonight.

The bus is an enormous, ancient vehicle that rumbles like the spaceship's engine. We climb up a set of steps, where Amara scans our tickets, then we find seats in the back among dozens of other humans. They all stare as I pass, and a few giggle or gasp. Soon the bus is moving again, and I nearly trip over myself.

Amara doesn't release my arm as we sit together, watching the city go by the windows. It's charming, I think, in its own way. The backwardness of humankind is almost endearing.

"We get off here," she says after a time, sitting up to pull a wire running along the windows. The bus slows, and she leads me out the back entrance.

Then we're standing on a street corner, and Amara seems even more excited as we head off, toward bright, flickering signs.

"Okay, so you're going to meet two people who are very important to me," she says, her expression turning serious. Well, as serious as it can be, given that she's Amara. "First, there's Marguerite. I've known her since freshman year of college. She's a little hoity-toity at first, but I promise, she's a whole bad bitch."

I can't tell if that's supposed to be a good or a bad thing, but I think it's a good thing.

"Next is Fiona. She seems sweet and happy, but she's also a bad bitch."

Okay, definitely being a *bad bitch* seems to be a good thing.

Amara giggles. "Both of them are super sweet. And they're excited to meet you."

I take a deep breath. I knew I'd have to meet my new wife's friends and family, but now it's upon us. Hopefully they'll find me to be a good match for Amara.

We reach a building with darkened windows, so it looks like there's nothing but blackness inside. A bright sign announces CLUB TENDRIL. We get in line behind a group of other people waiting to get in, each of them passing by a big strong woman dressed in a black jacket.

"Your visa," Amara says, nudging me. I pull the document from my pocket and produce it as we approach the jacketed woman.

Her eyes travel from my feet to my face, ending with a quirk of her brow when she notices my antennae.

"Nice boyfriend," she says to Amara. "Matching Program?"

"Yep! This is Roth'kar. He's a Karthinian."

I bring all my hands to my chest, close my eyes, and lift my chin in greeting.

"Ooh." The woman returns my visa. "Cute. Have fun."

Amara pulls me along through the door behind her, giggling.

"I think she liked you," she says with a wink. "Too bad for her, you're taken."

I believe Amara means that I'm with her and thus unavailable, so I nod in agreement. It gives me an odd but pleasant tickle in my chest.

Inside, the room is not as dark as it looked. Lights in all manner of bright colors swing around us, and flashes of white distract me. More humans than I can count are dancing underneath them to the beat of the intense music. It's fast-paced and wild, like the sound is everywhere all at once. I've never seen anything like this, with so many beings gathered in one place. None of the dank, narrow hallways or residential cubicles in the Hole are sized to hold monumental groups of people like this, not even the slophouse.

I thought it might feel crushing, but it is strangely freeing. I am just one of many in the crowd, all moving with a frenzied liberation that makes me envious. They are so carefree.

Amara leads me through the darkness by my lower right hand toward some humans standing behind a countertop.

"What can I get for you two?" asks a woman dressed all in black.

"Two gin and tonics." Amara whips out her wallet and provides her credit again. "Start a tab, please."

"You got it."

After ordering, Amara exchanges her wallet for her personal communicator, tapping out a message to one of her friends.

"Fiona says she's here. Marguerite is on the way." She tucks the device into her purse, scanning the crowd. She has given me one of my own, but besides saving her phone number in it, I have not given it much thought. It is rather archaic in design.

"Amara!" A tiny woman leaps out of nowhere, nearly bowling over Amara. The woman is short with cropped whitish-yellow hair and huge blue eyes. She pulls away long enough to notice me. "Oh, and the *husband*."

"Roth'kar," I say, offering my hand as humans do. She grins widely and takes it in hers, shaking vigorously.

"Fiona. Great handshake." She releases me and gives Amara an approving nod. "Firm. Good sign."

"You and signs." Amara laughs playfully. Then the woman behind the counter returns, sliding two drinks across it. Amara hands me one.

"Ready to get your first taste of Earthling alcohol?"

I nod, and we each take a sip. It's remarkably good, though strong. This is… clean. Smooth. Easy to drink.

I marvel at it as we meander away from the counter area, toward the dancing throng. Fiona leads us to a table nearby that happens to be open, and Amara and I sit in the booth together. There are so many other people that we're practically forced into each other's laps, and I have to put one set of arms around her back to make enough room.

Amara giggles and nestles into me, clearly reading my gesture as affectionate, not necessary. Fiona claps her hands.

"You two look happy together already," she says as I sip my drink again, enjoying the flavor.

"It's only been a day." Amara is smiling at me as she says it, though. "But I think we're off to a good start."

I nod in agreement, keeping the tiny straw in my mouth so I don't have to talk.

"There she is," Fiona says, getting to her feet. She waves to someone behind us. "Marguerite! Over here!"

A woman appears with long, jet-black hair, in black clothing, with her mouth set in a firm line. Amara gets to her feet, pulling me up along with her. She runs to her friend and they hug, though Marguerite's face doesn't change from its serious expression.

"So, you're the alien," she says, studying me. Something about her voice sounds... dangerous. For a split second, I wonder if someone has found me out. "I would love to get to know you better, *Roth'kar*."

CHAPTER NINE

AMARA

MARGUERITE IS INTENSE, I know that. Perhaps I should have warned Roth'kar better. She acts stuck-up and a little harsh, but deep down she's a softie. She loves Fiona and me dearly and would do anything for us.

Which is, perhaps, why it looks like she's hiding a knife as she gives Roth'kar the evil eye.

"So," she says, imperiously leaning forward on one hand, speaking loud enough that we can hear her over the music. She hasn't even ordered a drink yet. "What are your intentions with Amara?"

Roth'kar shifts in his seat. "I intend to be a good husband."

"You're not her *real* husband yet," Marguerite corrects. "I know you don't sign the official paperwork until the thirty days are up."

Roth'kar's antennae tense, shrinking down onto his head even though his face betrays nothing.

"I am not thinking of it that way." He straightens, still keeping his right arms around me. "I am committed to making this work."

"That sure sounds nice," Marguerite says, pouncing on him like a cat on a mouse. "But what happens if you and Amara fight about some cultural difference? Surely you'll have lots of those."

I stiffen. *Like kissing.* What if he truly never wants to do that? What if we don't even like the same things in bed?

"Marguerite," I hiss under my breath, because I don't like the doubt her questions are stirring in me. But Marguerite just waits for him to answer.

"I would like to think that we can talk out our differences." Roth'kar's tone is calm. "I am eager to learn more about Earth culture, as well as the flora and fauna. Your planet is very beautiful and diverse."

"He did pet some trees today," I chime in, and this causes Marguerite to arch an eyebrow.

"He what?"

"The trees are beautiful," Roth'kar says thoughtfully. "I've never seen anything like them."

"Why?" Marguerite's question is poised like a dagger. "Are there not trees where you come from?"

"He's from a spaceship," I butt in, trying to get her to retract her claws. "He's never even been on a planet before now."

This makes her squint with suspicion. "Interesting. How do you know you'll do all right on Earth, then?"

"I don't." Roth'kar connects eyes with hers. "It will be a new lesson every day, I imagine. And I will have to grow and adapt accordingly."

Marguerite's lips purse, but she settles back in her chair, arms crossed, as if she's decided to back off for now.

"Whew, now that the inquisition is over," Fiona jokes, slinging an arm around Marguerite's shoulders, "we should get you a drink, Margie, and then it's time for dancing!"

The two of them sidle off together toward the bar, leaving Roth'kar and me alone.

I exhale a long breath. "Sorry about that." I clasp the hand that's around my shoulders. "Marguerite is intense. I didn't know she'd jump on you like that, but—"

"It's all right." He offers me a smile. "I can handle it, Amara."

That's true. He did hold his own pretty well. I have to stop treating him like a child who can't defend himself.

Roth'kar takes a few more sips of his drink, and his antennae curl forward in what appears to be pleasure.

"I knew I might encounter friends and family of yours who are protective," he says. "That they may doubt what we have because it's so new—and our arrangement is rather unusual."

I relax a little, glad that we got through that introduction without too much bloodshed. Hopefully Marguerite will chill out for the rest of the night so we can have a good time.

I'm nearly finished with my drink by the time my friends get back, and I'm itching to get onto the dance floor.

"Do you want to go out there and dance?" I ask, gesturing to the crowd. Roth'kar's brows rise on his forehead as he studies the bodies moving chaotically, surging along with the pounding music.

"I don't know how to dance. This is not something Karthinians do."

I have trouble imagining anyone in the universe who doesn't dance. "How do you have fun?"

Roth'kar pauses. "With stories, mostly. About what life was like back on our planet." He shrugs. "Sometimes my friend Zono and I played betting games, but he's a schemer and usually won all my chips."

"Why?"

He gives me a deadpan look. "It is like trying to cheat a cricket of his money." When I shake my head, not under-standing the joke, he adds, "Crickets do not have money, Amara."

I snort, then stand up and offer my hand to Roth'kar.

"You don't need any experience to be able to dance. Dancing is just... how your body moves when you're feeling it."

He cocks his head, thinking over this. Then, reluc-tantly, he accepts and takes my hand in his.

I lead us out onto the floor, on the edge of the mass of bodies. Immediately, my feet and legs know what to do, driven by the beat. Roth'kar is standing stock-still, studying me as I dance.

"Try it," I call out over the noise, wiggling my butt more than I usually do. "Just let the music in. Let it tell you what to do."

Roth'kar closes his eyes, and the heavy bass rolls over us. His feet start to move in rhythm, which then leads to his legs. I put a hand on his hip, and his eyes fly open, but I don't let go as I apply pressure in time with the beat.

Soon, his hips are swaying, and I nod encouragingly. "There we go!"

I let him go once he's got some of the movements down, and we move near the dense group closer to the sound stage. Roth'kar doesn't miss the couple next to us —a woman dancing with her back against a man's front, their hips gyrating in perfect synchronicity. His mouth falls open, as if scandalized by it.

Okay, we won't try that, then.

Experimentally, I take one of his hands in mine and try to rock back and forth in the same tempo. In response, he winds our fingers together and starts moving even more of his body in sync with mine.

"Good!" I call out over the music. It's time to get down.

I shimmy and shake, using my hips and ass and knees. People are staring at us now, surprised by the alien in their midst. But Roth'kar ignores them, dancing along with me, still holding my hand. Those bright blue eyes of his are riveted on me, traveling from my face down to my feet, and then back again.

"You are beautiful tonight, Amara," he says, just loud enough I can hear him over the music.

It takes me by surprise. I didn't think he noticed.

"Thank you." Using our linked hands, I pull myself closer to him. "I did it for you."

Roth'kar's lips part in surprise. Then, a cautious smile comes over his face, and he reaches with his lower left hand to take mine, his upper hands gently resting on my shoulders. He doesn't say anything else, but he doesn't need to as the music swirls over us. Soon, Marguerite and Fiona join, and Roth'kar and I release our hold on one another so we can all dance together.

This is when we let loose. Fiona goes wild, dragging

over some woman she finds dancing alone in the mass around us so they can dance together. Marguerite is alone, as she always is, just enjoying the environment. Sometimes someone will ask her to dance, and she'll humor them for a couple of minutes before moving on.

After a while I need a drink, so I ask Roth'kar to leave the dance floor with me, and he eagerly agrees. We stock up on water, then head to the bar for our next round of drinks.

"How many are allowed?" he asks as we find a different place to sit at the bar now that our old seats are gone.

"Allowed?" I laugh. "Until you can't walk anymore, I guess. If you look too drunk or act belligerent, they'll stop serving you."

He nods thoughtfully. "That's reasonable." He looks down into his cup. "Does this cost you a lot? Taking me out like this?"

An odd question. "I suppose it adds up. But that's why I have a job I go to every day—so I can have fun when I go out. That's the point, baby!"

"But it will cost twice as much when you're with me," he points out.

"For twice the fun? Sounds like a good deal."

Now, he's actually, really smiling, and I feel like I've won a prize.

"You humans and your *deals*."

We both throw back our drinks, then Roth'kar spots Fiona in the crowd, and we dive back into the foray of dancers. We're holding hands as I push through the bodies in the way, and he follows along close behind me until we've reached Fiona and Marguerite again.

Now that we've reunited on the dance floor, Roth'kar is moving easier now, more naturally, so I slide my arm around his waist. He peers down at me, arching an eyebrow, but then his lower arm settles around my hip, too. His upper hand reaches up to lift a lock of my hair as we move in time with the beat, but he says nothing as he examines it.

He inhales, and he seems to like whatever it is that he smelled.

As the night goes on, people get more and more frisky, dancing dirty and making out. It warms me all over, wondering what it would be like to do that with Roth'kar. I don't want to push him, though—but maybe the next time we go out, we could get closer.

Then the music changes, and an even faster song comes on. Everyone in the crowd starts moving at once, and we're swept up in it. Fiona throws her hands in the air, so I do, too, and then Roth'kar does. We dance wildly, and for an alien who's never danced before, my new husband sure knows how to work it.

When the song's over, we take a break to get another drink. Roth'kar is enthused with gin and tonics, so I make sure to order him a third one, and we find some spare seats at the bar while we try to get our breath back.

"This is fun," Roth'kar says with obvious surprise. "This *clubbing* thing, it's very enjoyable."

Perfect. I lean back into his shoulder. He's stiff for a moment before he lets me come in closer. His hands curl around my side.

"I'm glad you're having fun," I say. "Next time, though, we'll pre-game, and that will be cheaper."

"Pre-game?"

"Start drinking before we come." I giggle. "Arrive already lubed up and ready to party."

"Did you two love birds ditch us?" Fiona calls out, popping up between us at the bar. "You were there one moment, gone the next."

I gesture to our drinks. "Have to stay topped up!"

Roth'kar holds up a single finger. "I believe she's right."

Fiona hoots. "You've already got him on your side, Amara. That's a good start."

After Marguerite has gotten her next drink, too, all of us find a nice place to sit and lounge until we have our energy back. Roth'kar is quiet, but remains with his arms around me, and I think Fiona's right.

This *is* a good start.

It's nearly one in the morning by the time we all say goodnight, and Roth'kar and I head for the bus stop. I loop my hand through his arm the whole way, even though both of us are unsteady on our feet after so many drinks.

"Good thing you don't have four legs," I say to Roth'kar as I stumble on a crack in the sidewalk, but he keeps me upright. I giggle. "Thanks."

"What would be wrong with four legs?" he asks, voice slurring slightly. I like that he also went wild tonight, and though he's steadier on his feet than I am, his eyes look glassy and he has a silly smile on his face. Well, as much of a smile as he seems capable of.

"This walking business would be harder, wouldn't it?" I snort. "Imagine trying to dance with four legs!"

Roth'kar nods seriously. "That would be difficult."

We come to a stop at the bus shelter and sit beside each other on the empty bench. We're the only people trying to take the 59 home at this time of night. I lean into Roth'kar's shoulder, pleased by his warmth, by his scent. I know he's not wearing any deodorant or cologne—since he doesn't have any—so it's just the smell of his sweat, but I like it. It's comforting and delicious, but maybe that's just the alcohol talking.

"Thanks for coming out with me tonight," I murmur as his two arms loop easily around my back. We grew closer this evening and got to know each other much better. I like what I've learned so far.

"It was a pleasure." Roth'kar rubs my shoulder with his upper hand. "I enjoyed seeing more of your life and meeting your friends."

"Aw." I snuggle in closer as cars pass. "They liked you, even if Marguerite was a little difficult at first."

I can feel Roth'kar smile as he leans his head down against mine. "I'm glad. I want your friends to like me."

"Well, I like you, too, for what it's worth."

Roth'kar's quiet, still holding me. I tilt my head to get a look at his face, and it's pensive.

"Tonight was very fun," he says, brows furrowed in a way that contradicts his words. "I have never had fun like that. Carefree and wild."

"You didn't have friends on the spaceship?" I ask, surprised.

"I did, of course. But... we did not have *fun* together. Not the way you do with Marguerite and Fiona." He still looks lost in thought. "It was a new experience for me to simply forget about everything else. In the Hole, hunger always gnaws at your insides. You sleep, and then wake, and then work, and then sleep again, sometimes eating in between. If you do not work, you do not eat."

The fog of easygoing pleasure around us fades. He had such a hard life before this, and he's clearly traumatized.

"The way your friends were with you, caring for you, looking out for you, interrogating me to make sure I am a good match for you?" Roth'kar chuckles as if this is a fond memory. "Most of my friendships were ones of convenience. If something went wrong, I could not depend on them the way you depend on your friends."

"That won't be your life again," I assure him. "You're with me now, and we'll always have food to eat. You can always depend on me."

This time, his voice is quieter. "Thank you, Amara."

"You don't have to thank me. It's my job as your wife." I still like how that word tastes. "I'll always be here for you."

We fall into a companionable silence again as we wait for the bus. They come far more infrequently this late at night, and I'm glad that, for once, I'm not waiting alone.

"I saw lots of people doing the *kissing*," Roth'kar suddenly says. He tilts his head to look down at me. "On Earth, this is how you show someone you like them?"

"It's one way. There are lots of ways." I turn so I'm facing him on the bench. "We could find other ways if you don't like that one."

"But it's a way *you* like." It's not a question.

I'm just drunk enough that I say, "Yeah. I really like it." Maybe my dry spell has lasted more than half a decade now, but I still remember how exciting and intoxicating it was to just make out against a wall, rubbing bodies together, building up the tension for what might happen later—

Roth'kar leans down so our faces are even closer together. I lick my lips, moistening them, wondering if he's going to do what I'm hoping he's going to do.

His blue eyes still wide open, my alien places his lips on mine.

CHAPTER TEN

ROTH'KAR

I HAVE no idea what I'm doing, unfortunately, but the alcohol has made me bold enough to attempt it. My mouth is on hers, and nothing is happening while I stare at her and she stares back at me. It's not as repulsive as I expected, but nothing pleasurable, either.

Suddenly, Amara giggles against my mouth.

"Close your eyes," she whispers, sliding closer to me on the bench. Our mouths are still mostly touching.

Obediently, I close my eyes. Then Amara's lips travel over mine, as if she's exploring me, and I try not to move so she can complete her circuit.

She laughs again. "Roth'kar. A kiss is a two-way street." I don't know what she means by this, but I get the sense she wants me to reciprocate in some way. So I imitate her motion, trying to get a sense of the shape of her mouth using mine. Her lips are giving, molding around me, pressing back occasionally before letting me continue.

I sense that this is a sort of dance, too, but an intimate kind. Amara grows bolder, this time sucking my lower lip in between hers, and my body unexpectedly jolts. That felt… good. Strangely good.

Amara lets out a *hmm* sound, then repeats the motion with my upper lip. I have never considered my mouth to be an erogenous zone, but my culans lift, fueled by our act.

Then her tongue comes out. It licks briefly along my lip, surprising me, but I'm careful not to pull away.

I did not realize our tongues would be involved with this, too. That was not in the image the translator provided me.

The swipe of that wet appendage a second time makes my culans engorge even further, and I shove my hand down against them to keep them from sprouting upright. Immediately I imagine Amara running that tongue over their sensitive ridges the way she's doing with my lips, and my mouth parts, my own tongue responding.

"Mmm," Amara says against me as we meet in the middle.

I didn't intend to do it, but she instantly melts against me, her lips sinking deeper into mine. Now the tips of our tongues are greeting, twining as we remain fully joined. When I thrust my tongue into her mouth, I expect a reproach, but instead Amara moans in a way that's distinctly erotic. Her hand tangles in my hair as she pulls me even closer, and I tumble into this *kissing*.

I think I understand it now. It is a dance, yes, but also a tease. It is intimacy and touch, it is closeness and affection, just as much as it is a hint at lust. It is so many things, and gross is not even at the top of my list.

Finally, I find myself struggling for breath, so I pull away. Amara is staring at me with huge, dark eyes, her lips parted as she also tries to bring in air.

That is when the bus rumbles along. Unsteadily I get to my feet, then help Amara up, too. She presents the driver with our tickets, and we stumble to the back as the bus starts moving again.

"Wow," she says into my ear as I sit next to her. "You're good at that."

I'm shocked, given it was my first time.

"Did you like it?" I ask, finding that I want even more of her praise, to know if I pleased her and met her expectations.

"Oh, I did." She winds our fingers together in her lap. "I definitely did."

The ride home is a blur. All I remember is our hands linked together and Amara's voice as she narrates where we're going, what landmarks we're passing.

Then we get off at our stop. I stray away from her, to what I think is our way home, and she grabs my arm, laughing. "Not that way. There are no streetlights that way."

I blink up at the lights overhead.

"They keep us safe at night," she says. "Don't wander off down dark alleys."

I take note of that, wondering what might lurk on the streets where there are no lights. Perhaps squirrels. Or worse, *dogs*. I can't have Amara getting bitten by an animal on my watch.

When we reach a corner, she tries to step out into the

street while the light is red. I grab her by the arm and hold her back.

"It is not time." I point at the orange hand sign.

Amara obediently stops beside me. "Of course, Dad," she says with a giggle. I don't know what this means, as I am not her father, but she is also drunk.

It is… adorable.

When the walking man appears, I lead her across the street to make sure she doesn't trip, and she holds onto me all the way home.

Back in the apartment, Amara convinces me to drink two whole glasses of water, then bids me goodnight and toddles off to her room alone, muttering something to herself. Now I know what *getting wasted* entails.

I am tempted to follow her. Not because I intend anything lewd, but because I worry about her well-being. If I were next to her, I could keep an eye on her. But she did not invite me and so I go back to my own room with the *futon*.

I don't mind sleeping here, but as my vision swims, I think it might be pleasant if I weren't by myself. I spent all night at Amara's side, watching as her makeup smudged and her smile grew wider, and I want to keep watching. I wonder what she looks like as she sleeps.

When I close my eyes, the world is still tilting and swaying in the blackness, but I'm so exhausted that I'm swept away.

"Roth'kar!" The sound of my name being called out worms its way into my consciousness.

I sit up, bleary-eyed, on the too-small bed. A steady, low thrumming in my head makes every vibration hurt, including the knock on the door to my room.

"Coffee?" Amara asks quietly.

I squint. "Co—what?"

The door opens as I rub my painful head, and Amara slips inside. She has a mug full of something steaming hot, and a tangy but pleasant smell fills the air.

"Coffee," she repeats. "It's a drink that will help with your hangover."

"Hangover?" I reach for the hot mug and Amara gently places it in my hands, patting my arm. I sniff the dark liquid, and the scent is foreign but delicious.

"That nasty feeling you have in your head and your stomach right now." She gives me a pitying look. "It's called a hangover. I'm not doing much better. That's how I know."

I bring the drink to my lips and sip. I'm taken aback at how bitter it is, and I push the mug away.

"Disgusting," I say, running my tongue over my teeth to clear away the flavor. Amara laughs.

"You'll change your mind." She takes my hand in hers and tugs. "Eating something will help you feel better. Come on, there's bacon cooking."

I don't know what this *bacon* is, but as I reluctantly leave my room, I smell it: something fatty and salty and smoky. My mouth waters.

"It's almost done." Amara scurries to the kitchen, flipping food over in a pan. "Plus eggs and some orange juice. The perfect hangover cure."

While I sit at the table, she plates the meal, then carries it over and sets it down in front of me, followed by a cup of some kind of... sure enough, orange-colored juice.

"How literal," I remark as I take a sip. This is much more acceptable than the *coffee*.

Amara giggles, and I'm surprised by how upbeat she is, given neither of us are feeling our best. She looks happy, even though there are bags under her eyes.

I dive into the food, and I discover bacon is a revelation. It's salty—a flavor we had very little of on *New Dro'thar II*—and fatty in the most sublime way. I've never had anything like it, and I feel healed by it. I moan as I obliterate the four pieces she's put on my plate, and Amara giggles.

"You like it?"

"I do not think that's a strong enough word," I say, chewing.

Though the bacon is delicious, I am wary of the white substance with the yellow center.

"Chicken egg," Amara explains. "It's pure protein. Make sure you eat it all, and it'll help."

I bite into the egg, and though the texture is strange, I don't mind the flavor. When my food is gone, and Amara has finished hers, she spreads out on her chair, nearly melting to the floor.

"That's all I had in me," she moans.

"Don't worry. I'll clean." This time, Amara doesn't object as I take care of the plates, rinsing and loading them into the dish-cleaning machine I saw her use last time. After scrubbing the pans, I return to find Amara has migrated to the couch, sprawling across it. She lifts her legs to make room for me, and then when I'm seated, sets them back down on my lap.

It is casual in its intimacy, and a warmth spreads across my body.

She turns on a movie, which is a struggle for me to follow, but it's simply enjoyable to lie here and let my food digest. As she predicted, I do feel better by the middle of the day, but make sure to drink more of that orange juice.

I don't realize when I fall asleep.

The sun is down by the time I open my eyes, and Amara is gone.

I sit up, suddenly panicked by her absence. She was here earlier, but...

The front door opens, and Amara steps inside with a plastic bag hanging from her arm. She grins when she sees me.

"Oh, good. You're up. Feel better?" She sets the bag down on the table. "I got us takeout."

The flavors are unusual, the smells alluring. She explains that it's "Chinese food," and though I try to use the *chopsticks* that come with it, I find it too impossible in my half-asleep state. After gorging on the food, we find our way back to the couch.

This time, when I sit on it, she sits close to me. I think of our *kissing* last night at the bus stop, and wonder if she is, too. She leans against me, and so I put two of my arms around her, bringing her in tighter to my chest.

We sit like that for some time as the television prattles on, but I'm not paying attention to it. Amara smells different today now that all the artificial scents she put on last night have worn off. I like her natural musk—it reminds me of something familiar. Perhaps it's a little like my mother before she died.

Amara's hand traces up my shoulder to my neck, where she plays with the short strands of my hair.

"What are you thinking about?" she asks.

"My mother."

The words just come out, honest and true. I think my headache has eliminated my filter.

"Your mother? Is she back on the ship you came from?" Amara cocks her head. "I haven't asked you about your family."

"I have none."

Her hand freezes. "None at all?"

"My mother and father both died in my young adult-hood. I have no siblings. I have two aunts and an uncle, but we don't speak much." One of my aunts worked her way up to a slightly better job on the second rung of the ship, cleaning quarters for wealthier people, so I never saw her. The rest of us were too consumed with simply trying to get by in the Hole to spend much time together, and we live in vastly different places. *New Dro'thar II* is the larger of the two ships that hold our entire civilization, and getting from one side of the Hole to the other is a long journey.

"Oh. I'm so sorry." Her hand resumes playing with my hair, and Amara is gazing at me now with soft eyes. "That sounds difficult."

"It is what I know."

"You have a new family now, though." She smiles at me, snuggling in closer. "You have me."

Something gnaws at my insides at these words. *Family.* She truly feels that way about me?

I know this sensation in my gut—guilt. Guilt that I only came here to escape that life, not thinking of who I would meet on the other end. I am lucky it was she. But I should have come here as eager to be her companion as she was eager to have me.

"What about you?" I ask her, trying to change the course of my thoughts. "Will I meet your parents?"

"Eventually. Well, just my mom. My dad died when RVS hit."

Right. The plague that decimated the male population of Earth.

"I'm sorry." I rub her shoulder.

She shrugs. "It's okay. I was really little. Mom's somewhere in the Caribbean right now. I told her I was applying to the Matching Program, but I'm not sure if she heard me over the music." Amara rolls her eyes. "She's always on a cruise of some kind. I haven't seen her in probably two years."

It sounds like Amara does not have much of a family, either. Sympathetic, I pull her in closer.

"Then I will be your family, too," I say. Maybe I cannot undo how I entered this relationship, but I can certainly decide how I continue it.

Tipping up Amara's chin with my hand, I kiss her.

CHAPTER ELEVEN

AMARA

OH, wow. It's clear that Roth'kar wasn't too drunk last night to remember our kissing lessons, because he brings out his new skills and uses them on me with exacting force. He caresses my lips with his, teasing them and hinting what else he could do. I slide both hands around his neck, letting myself fall into him as our kiss becomes more and more.

Then he tastes me with his tongue, and I'm a goner. At the speed of light, we leap from *kissing* to *making out*, fully diving in. Perhaps this is how my new alien husband will open up to me.

I caress the side of his face as we kiss deeper, tongues twining, teeth nipping and lips never relenting. Roth'kar's other set of arms curls around my side, and one of his hands travels up my back, under my hair. He groans into me as he runs his fingers through it, then cups the back of my head.

Now that he's sober, it's time to take this up a notch.

Not breaking the kiss, I slide into Roth'kar's lap, and his whole body convulses underneath me. He breaks away for a moment, his eyes big.

"Amara...?"

"Too soon?" I ask, moving to leave. But his grip on me halts my progress.

"No." He pushes some hair away from my face, tucking it behind my ear. "Not at all. Just... surprised."

"Good surprised?"

"Good surprised."

That's what I like to hear. Settling back into the nest of his thighs, I'm pleased to find a distinct lump in his pants. *Good surprised, indeed.*

Making out is easier in this position, and I love how Roth'kar has so many hands with which to touch me. Does he realize how his palms have roamed down my hips and then up again, like he's mapping me out? He's fully focused on kissing me, invading my mouth with his lips and tongue, and I return it just as eagerly.

That lump under his pants has grown significantly by the time I come up for air. Roth'kar rests his forehead against mine, and he's panting, too.

"Now that we have done the kissing, like you suggested, is it time to take off my clothing?"

His question takes me by surprise. Is he ready to go to the next level? Am *I* ready for that?

"Oh, um." I'm still drunk on our make-out session, so it takes a moment for my brain to catch up. He is my husband, after all. I like him, I find him attractive, and... again, he's my husband.

But something about his question doesn't feel right.

"It's only time if you want it to be," I say. "We can just keep doing this, too."

Roth'kar studies me, like he's trying to understand the words I'm not saying.

"What would make you most comfortable, Amara?" he asks. "You are my wife, and so I believed intercourse is expected. But I only want to do what you want to do."

Expected? That word sends a shiver down my spine, and I reflexively pull away, returning to my own seat on the couch. Roth'kar lets me go, but his antennae wilt as I put distance between us.

"I don't expect anything from you." A cold shiver runs down my back. "Whatever happens between us, I want it to be something we both desire equally. Not because we feel like it's required."

Roth'kar shifts, as if he's unsettled. "As your husband, I want to satisfy you."

He feels obligated by our marriage? I don't like this at all. What if we've only been kissing because he feels like it's required?

"You are not thinking pleasant thoughts," he observes. It must show on my face how terrible that idea feels.

"No, I'm not. I'm wondering if… if you even want to do this." I curl my hand protectively at my chest. "If you want to be here at all."

Roth'kar's brows furrow. "Here, with you? Of course I do. I traveled a long way because…" He hesitates. "Because I wanted to be with you."

"And the kissing?" I ask, my voice coming out small and strained.

His eyes widen. "That is what's on your mind?" He strokes my shoulder with his upper hand, and unconsciously, I lean into him. "You don't think I want to kiss you?"

I nod, unable to speak.

"Amara." He sighs deeply. "I have enjoyed all our time together. I kissed you because I wanted to kiss you. I can assure you of this."

"I don't want to be an obligation to you."

Now that I think about it, how could I not be? Sure, he came here of his own volition—he didn't need to sign up for the Matching Program—but I would feel obligated, were I in his position. If my partner were buying my clothes and taking me out for a night on the town...

Roth'kar's voice is firm, his expression hard and unyielding as he says, "Stop, Amara."

I blink up at him, surprised by this new, more forceful Roth'kar, who I haven't seen before. He faces me, taking both of my hands in his lower ones, then placing the upper ones on my shoulders.

"You are not an obligation," he says firmly. "You are a joy. I did not know what to expect when I came to Earth, and I am glad—more than glad—that my bride turned out to be you. That is the only reason I want to please you. Because I have come to care for you, and truthfully, I want you to care for me, too."

"Oh, I do!" The words burst out of me. "I do care about you, Roth'kar. And you don't have to kiss me or take your clothes off for me for that to be true."

He smiles an unsteady smile. "But what if I want to do those things?"

"Then..." A little bolt of electricity shoots through me. "Then we can. If you really want to."

Instead of answering, Roth'kar slides his many arms

around me, drawing me back into our bubble of closeness from before. He runs one hand through my hair and closes his eyes.

"I've wanted to touch your hair since last night." He bites his lip as he combs his fingers between the strands. "It is just as lovely as I imagined."

It's romantic and sensual, and surprising. "Since last night?"

Roth'kar nods, pulling me closer to him so I can't see his face as he strokes my hair. "When you emerged from the bathroom, ready to go out, I was enthralled by your hair."

I gasp as his mouth drifts down to my neck, and I can feel his breath against my skin.

"I didn't realize you liked it."

"Oh, I did. Very much. And that dress." One of his hands has gone exploring southward, and it gently squeezes my ass. "It looked marvelous on you. Like it was made for you."

That spark of electricity is growing and spreading the more he touches me, the more he talks to me.

"But..." He pauses, then presses a chaste kiss to the flesh of my neck. When did I teach him necking? He must have figured that one out on his own. "Perhaps it is too soon. Perhaps I am rushing us when you aren't quite ready."

My face gets hot. I don't want him to stop, but at the same time, we've only lived together for a few days. We hardly know each other, and I'm sure that's why I felt so uncertain tonight.

"All right." I sit back on my heels, separating us, because with the scent of him so close, I want more of him. "Clothes on, I guess. For now."

Roth'kar kisses me, a gentle, slow kiss that's just his soft lips against mine. Then he withdraws, stroking my cheek.

"For now."

We stay huddled together on the couch after that, so I grab a throw and we flip on a movie. It's a romantic comedy, and even though Roth'kar doesn't get all the jokes, when the leads kiss, he pulls me in against his side and leans his cheek on the top of my head.

I'm glad I signed up for an alien husband. I hope we can get closer the more days we have together, because I want him. I relish all of his kisses, all of his touches, and I need even more of them when the time is right.

Once we head to our separate rooms, I lie awake in bed, my body disappointed that we didn't go further tonight. It's been so long since I've had that kind of close-ness with anyone that I'm craving it, starving for it.

Hmm. I bring my wand out of my bedside table and shove it under the blankets before turning it on, hoping it doesn't make too loud of a noise. The vibration against my clit is heavenly, and I gasp and bite my lip while my plea-sure rises. I close my eyes, thinking of Roth'kar's arms around me, his mouth on mine, and hold in a moan. I can't stop fantasizing about what might be under those leggings of his, how it would feel if he were on top of me, thrusting in and out of me.

It's easy to finish, and I cover my mouth as my orgasm tears through me.

Woof. Roth'kar has me hot and bothered. I know it will take some time to work up to that level together, but I can't wait.

Unfortunately, the following day is a workday, and then it's time to go grocery shopping. I consider suggesting to Roth'kar that he stay home, but I remember he doesn't want me to baby him, so I offer that we go together.

He is amazed by the grocery store. "There are so many choices," he says as I search for the brand of spices I want.

"Too many. Sometimes you can't decide."

"I could never decide," he agrees.

I plan a few different meals that I think he'll like—curry and spaghetti—and plan on going out to eat at least one night. I'll have to be a little more budget-conscious with another mouth to feed, especially one that eats as much as Roth'kar does, but a meal out once a week shouldn't hurt.

Roth'kar gets many stares in the store, and a few people bump into him without realizing it, then let out little gasps when they realize who he is. A little girl points him out and asks her mother, "Is that an alien?"

The mother looks at me for confirmation before saying, "Yes, honey, that's an alien."

Overall, it's an uneventful trip, but Roth'kar looks shell-shocked when we get in the car.

"So many people," he says, grinding his teeth. "And so…"

"Frustrating?"

"They would stop and speak in the middle of an aisle!" He raises his arms in the air. All four of them. "Why not stop and speak somewhere else? At home, perhaps?"

I giggle as we drive back to the condo. It felt oddly

wonderful to do something as normal—and annoying—as going to the grocery store together.

One advantage to four arms is that Roth'kar can carry all the groceries in their reusable bags while I fiddle with the lock.

While we're cooking, he finds excuses to touch me now that he knows better how to help. He can bring me butter and oil, salt and pepper, though the extensive array of spices in the lazy Susan intimidates him. His hands travel over my back as he passes behind me, and I'm thrilled at this new version of him.

That night, before bed, I stop in front of Roth'kar's door as he uses his nifty little teeth-cleaning device.

"I need to get me one of those," I say. "Way smarter than a toothbrush."

"Indeed. I think they are fairly standard around the galaxy. I am surprised a Frahma has not tried to sell you one yet."

I burst out laughing. I guess I'm not the only one who clocked the little turtle aliens for what they are.

"Maybe you can get me the hookup to the cool alien gear," I say as he comes out to stand in the doorway.

"I would always lend you this one." He leans down, his lips only a few inches from mine. "Now that we have done this *kissing*, I suppose it wouldn't be that odd."

I stick out my tongue. "Sharing a toothbrush sounds weirdly gross."

He laughs, and then I'm closing the distance between

us, and now we're making out against the doorframe. My hands are all over Roth'kar's body and his hands are all over me, and suddenly I really want to strip his clothes off.

Taking a deep breath, I slow us down and bring myself back to Earth again. Our mouths separate, but our bodies remain tangled.

"Sleep well, Amara," Roth'kar says, finally releasing me from his embrace.

I step back out into the hallway, waving goodbye. "Goodnight."

CHAPTER TWELVE

ROTH'KAR

OH, are my culans hungry after so much kissing. Sinking my tongue into Amara's warm mouth made me think of what else I could put inside her, how it might feel to bury myself in that hot channel that my communicator tells me is between Amara's legs.

I did not intend to become so infatuated with my new wife, but I suppose it's not unwelcome. Perhaps once the trial is over and we secure my citizenship, it would be easiest to remain with her.

Once upon a time I had a friend who lived in the room beside mine and visited my bed often. But life in the Hole means all relationships are relationships of convenience. We sated our physical needs because we couldn't sate any others, and we fought frequently. I was attracted to her, and we had formed a close relationship, but when she had to relocate for work, I was only despondent for a short while.

How I'm beginning to feel about Amara, though? It is new. Different. Exciting, yet comforting. And her smell? How that scent has begun to drive me wild.

Of its own volition, my hand drifts down under my belt and pulls down my leggings, just enough to free my culans of their prison. This is the second time I've touched myself while thinking about Amara, and I wonder what sort of magic she carries with her that does this to me.

At first, my culans spread as they fill with blood, each flexing their ridges before clasping back together again. Then I wrap my hand around them firmly and squeeze, imagining them buried in Amara's singular passage.

I topple backward on the bed as I drag my hand up and down roughly, the soft teeth of my culans fluttering wildly. Once more, I think about how they would feel inside her, if they would please her. I love the sounds she makes as I kiss her, and I hope she will make more of them as I pleasure her.

When I near my finish, my culans clasp tightly together as I erupt. They part and spray out in two directions, and I hastily cover them with my hands so I can control the flow. I should have brought in a towel first.

I know my hand doesn't compare to what might await me in Amara's bed, but it will do for now.

The next morning, I make sure to be up before Amara leaves for work. She gives me my own key to the apartment and a kind of money I haven't seen before.

"Cash," she explains. "Not credit. This is one hundred and sixty dollars. Hopefully it will last you a bit."

I stare at the money, which is strangely the most familiar thing about this place. The Hole operated on a chip currency, where we were paid in chips of varying sizes and weights. These bills work the same way, with different numbers on them.

"Got it," I say, sweeping up the money and putting it in my pocket.

Amara gives me a sad smile, then gets up on her toes to kiss me. I return it eagerly, but I know she needs to leave for work, so I do not press for what I really want.

"I'll see you tonight." She wiggles her butt and departs.

My mind is so occupied with her after she leaves that I pull out my communicator once more and read through the Human Fact Sheet. I pay special attention to the diagrams, and they fuel the growing heat in my belly that is becoming familiar when I think about Amara.

Suddenly, I receive a message. Curious about who would want to contact me, I scroll down to it. It's from Zono, the Karthinian who lived in the room next to mine in our cubicle. We met working on a cleaning crew once, tasked with unclogging sewer drains. There is nothing like being covered in shit to build camaraderie. We couldn't get the stench out of our noses for days, but Zono always made a joke out of it, saying that at least we got a break from the smell of *kath*.

I don't even open it. Just thinking about the Hole fills me up with a nervous energy. I came here to escape that place, and I have been lucky enough to find Amara on the other side. But the sight of Zono's message

SO I MARRIED AN ALIEN

reminds me of the pretenses under which I came to Earth.

I thought I would come and use Amara to get what I wanted. Knowing what I know about her now... I don't want to think about the version of me who first came here.

So I put the communicator away instead.

To distract myself, I flip on the television. I am rather infatuated with this big flat-screen, though it seems to play mostly mindless nonsense. We had holo-vids in the Hole, but you used them almost exclusively for video communication and sending messages. People made recordings and shared them, but that was it. Holo-vids don't compare at all to the mountain of content available on the TV.

I scroll through it, trying out different shows. There are frequent breaks—usually at the worst moment—when suddenly, a man will appear on-screen, cleaning dishes and telling me all about the benefits of soap. These interruptions are the most confusing, as they are rarely related to the item being advertised. Sometimes there's no advertisement at all, and people simply run through open meadows hand in hand while an obnoxious voice lists of fifteen possible side-effects at top speed.

After a while of this mindless scrolling, I give up and decide to go on a walk to the park. At the entrance, I come across a cart with an incredible smell emanating from it. The woman behind the cart calls me over.

"Alien!" Her mouth forms an O. "Incredible! I've never seen an alien before."

"I cannot say you're my first human," I respond, gesturing at all the other humans around us.

The woman guffaws. "How'd you end up on Earth?"

"I married an Earthling."

Her brows go up. "Are you one of those mail-order husbands?" She fishes around in a bucket of hot water and pulls out a brown tube, which she then puts on a hot grill top.

"Mail-order?"

"Yeah. You came with the Galactic Matching Program?"

Ah, that's what she means. "That is how I got here, yes."

The woman turns the tube—which smells marvelous—to even out the grill marks. "Do you like it on Earth?"

"I believe so. It is... a vast improvement over where I come from."

Fresh sky, warm sun, and a cool breeze? I will never, ever take these gifts for granted.

"Hmm." The woman behind the cart pulls out some white bread and tosses it on the grill, too. "And your wife?"

How do I feel about Amara? I certainly like her. "She is a good woman. Works hard but likes to have fun." The more I talk about her, the more enthused I feel. "She is very generous and kind. To a fault, perhaps."

The woman cocks her head. "You sound smitten."

I become aware of just how much I've said, and I bite my lip. The woman opens up the bread bun and drops the brown tube inside, then hands it to me. I take it, unsure of what it is or when I ordered it.

"Five bucks," she says.

"Bucks?" My translator supplies an image of a four-legged beast with horns.

"Dollars?" she clarifies.

"Oh, yes." Right—money. "Here you are." I pull out the bill marked with a five and pass it over to her, though I am fairly certain I never asked for... whatever this is.

"Enjoy," she says. "Be good to that wife of yours."

I give a nod to show I understand, then continue on my way, peering down at the food in my hands.

Well, it smells good. Might as well try it.

After my revelation of a lunch, I check out more of the neighborhood and try not to accidentally buy anything else. Then I head back to the apartment to watch some more television before Amara returns home.

It is strange, I must admit, not working all day long. I'm used to constantly being busy, unless there's a dry spell in odd jobs, in which case we tended to play a lot of chip games. It is a welcome relief to rest, but after so much of it, I'm not sure what to do with myself here.

Finally, Amara appears, and I'm overjoyed. I didn't expect what a rush I'd feel seeing her after being on my own all day, but I give her space as she comes in the door and sets down her jacket and purse. Once she's inside, I swoop down to kiss her.

"Oh!" She smiles against my mouth, and so I kiss her deeper, until she's falling into my arms.

I sure do like this kissing business. In fact, I get lost in it, my hands holding her soft body against mine, our lips tasting each other and our tongues playing between us. I can't get enough of her. She is far better than the brown tube in the bun.

At last, Amara giggles and pulls away.

"I'm happy to see you, too," she says with a wink, and I think just how charming she is as she swirls off to make dinner. "It's taco night. I hope you're ready!"

"Ah, yes, of the Taco Tuesdays?"

Amara beams. "Exactly!"

I help her as best I can, watching and learning everything she does so I can do my best to emulate it. In the future, perhaps I can have dinner ready for her when she gets home.

That night, we turn on a movie again, but we do what Amara calls "making out" instead of watching it. She sits astride my lap once more, and my culans rise, eager to be let out. But I keep them where they belong, simply enjoying her with my hands and lips, curious where they will lead me next.

A few days later, my new clothes are ready. Amara flings open the front door and brings them inside with her, absolutely ecstatic.

"Try these on and then let's go pick you up some new pants!"

Each garment is folded neatly inside a paper bag, and when I pick them up, I'm surprised by the quality. We use synthetic fabrics on *New Dro'thar II*, but these appear to be natural ones, soft but sturdy and thick.

The top item is a deep, dark blue with lighter blue trim

around the collar and sleeves. I eagerly head into the bathroom to change, as I don't think Amara is ready for me to walk around "bare-assed." I leave my leggings on, then strip off the stained, torn robe that came here with me. The moment I have these new *pants*, I'm going to throw my old clothing in the garbage.

I put on the shirt, and I'm pleased to find four holes exactly the right size and shape for my arms, and the collar sits neatly at the base of my throat. The image I see reflected back in the mirror is... strange. That Karthinian doesn't look, well, Karthinian anymore. It's an odd sight, seeing myself dressed like a human, but one I don't mind at all.

When I emerge from the bathroom, Amara leaps to her feet.

"Oh! You look amazing!" She rushes over to pet the new shirt. "Try on the next one!"

So we do this with all seven shirts, which come in dark blue, light blue, dark gray, white, brown and purple. All simple colors, Amara points out, that will be easy to coordinate.

Next, we're off to the clothing store, which is a shock to my system. Amara worried about the club when she should have worried about this "department store," which appears to be an emporium of options. There are clothes absolutely everywhere, in all manner of colors and sizes.

"Too many choices," I murmur to myself as we walk past rack after rack. How is one supposed to choose anything?

Eventually, we find the pants, and I try on a few pairs made from a starchy, unforgiving blue fabric that Amara calls "jeans." I don't care for them, but she likes the way they look, so I give them a try.

"Dang," she says when I come out wearing a pair with my new dark blue shirt. Her eyes are as big as saucers. "You look fire in those."

I preen, glad that she likes them. I pick a handful of them in different shades before she introduces me to the "sweatpants."

Oh, do I like the sweatpants. I will happily sit on the couch and watch television in them. I buy two pairs because I have a hard time imagining I'll want to wear these stiff "jeans" unless we're going out on the town, as Amara calls it.

After we check out, I wear the jeans home, and my wife finds excuses to touch my butt as we walk. I'm pleased that she likes it, as starchy as these new pants are.

Today, for the first time, I'm beginning to feel like an Earthling.

CHAPTER THIRTEEN

AMARA

WOW. I didn't think seeing Roth'kar in tight jeans and a form-fitting shirt would make me quite so hot to trot, but here we are. All the way home, I resist the urge to glance over at him, because I know it makes him nervous when I'm not always looking at the road.

"What do you think of going out tonight?" I ask as I pull into the parking garage. "Having a date night?"

Roth'kar cocks his head as he unbuckles his seatbelt. "Date... night?" He squints the way he always does when his translator is working.

"Like we go out together to a restaurant, have a nice dinner, and it's all very romantic." I swoon as I get out of the car. "There's a pretty nice place downtown that I like, but I don't go there much." I don't really have anyone to go with. Occasionally, Kendall and I have stopped by for drinks after work, but I always spied on others on dates with envy.

"Romantic," Roth'kar repeats as we get into the elevator, carrying bags of clothes with us. "I'm not sure how to do this. The translator is supplying me images of candles and red flowers."

I laugh. "Roses, probably. It's a tradition to sprinkle rose petals around when you're trying to seduce someone."

Roth'kar furrows his brow. "You decapitate flowers and spread around their remains to show love?"

"Uh, I guess you could say that. But the candles are about the lighting. You want the right kind of lighting when you're... you know."

"I do not know."

"When you're going to have sex," I say in a quieter voice. "Enough to see by, but not bright. Sexy lighting."

"Sexy... lighting." Roth'kar appears even more perplexed now. "But it is a fire hazard."

I giggle as we exit the elevator and head down the hall to my apartment. "I guess you're right. It's about the mood."

He ponders this as we step inside. "So a 'mood' is important during intercourse?"

The word *intercourse* nearly busts me up, but I hold my laugh inside because I don't want to embarrass him.

"Yes. You want to think sexy thoughts, not 'the light is too bright' thoughts."

He nods, understanding, then picks up his bags and heads to his room. I realize he doesn't have a closet or a dresser in there, and I kick past me for not thinking to get him one.

"Do you... do you want to put them in my room?" I

call after him, and Roth'kar pauses. "I can free up some drawers for you. And closet space."

He pivots, shooting me a surprised look.

"If it's not an imposition," he says carefully. "I don't want to encroach on your—"

"Oh, shush." I cross the distance between us and snatch the clothing bag from his hand. "Come on. We'll get you set up."

I made sure we bought him plenty of underwear and socks, too, so I free up two drawers for him—one for his pants and one for the unmentionables. The shirts I hang up in the closet next to mine.

"Is this okay?" I ask him, gesturing at the shirts.

Roth'kar appears perplexed by my question. "Why wouldn't it be? Now they won't get damaged or wrinkled."

"Well, you'll have to come into my room to get them, and…"

He arches an eyebrow when I don't finish my sentence. Roth'kar takes a step toward me, then another step, until we're almost chest to chest. Then he scoops up one of my hands with his lower arm and twines our fingers together.

"Yes, I will. And your room smells like you, which is a scent I very much enjoy."

Wow. Roth'kar has really opened up to me the last few days, and I'm more than grateful. I'm starting to see the real him inside, and that real him is surprisingly flirty and romantic.

"Well, we'd better get dressed if we want to get dinner," I say, pecking him on the cheek before I start rifling through the closet. He nods, chooses a shirt and a pair of pants, and then departs the room so I can change.

When I'm finally made up and ready, we head out together. Luckily, it's only a single bus trip to get downtown, and I made sure to call ahead for a reservation. We're running a little late, so we jog together down the street to the stop, arriving just before the bus rolls up.

We don't talk much on the way, sitting with our hands linked, my head resting on Roth'kar's shoulder. I pull the wire when we reach our stop, and we hop off the bus together.

Roth'kar's lips part in surprise as he takes in our new surroundings. Here, the buildings are huge and tall, jutting up into the sky so far they block out the setting sun.

"The restaurant is up there," I say, pointing at the top of a skyscraper. "You can look out the windows over the whole city."

Roth'kar's eyes get even bigger as he cranes his neck back to see.

"Come on." I loop my hand around his arm. "Let's eat."

We step into the lobby, then take the elevator up to the very top floor. When the doors open, we're greeted by the hum of restaurant noise—people talking and laughing, waiters stacking plates, and a gentle music playing. A woman glances up from the host stand as we approach, and her brows jump when she notices Roth'kar.

"Oh, hello!" She claps her hands together. "A Karthinian!"

Now it's our turn to be surprised.

"You know what he is?" I ask.

"Yes! Oh my gosh, it's so cool to meet you in person." The hostess is focused solely on Roth'kar, as if I'm not even there. She shyly extends a hand to him, and he pauses for a moment before he takes it and shakes.

"What deal are we making now?" he whispers to himself.

"I've been fascinated with aliens ever since the Frahma landed," the hostess barrels on. "I've read about Karthinians before but never seen one in real life!"

I tighten my hold on Roth'kar's arm as she finally releases his hand, but she's still going.

"Well, let me tell you, the food here is a lot better here than those *kath* bars you guys have."

Roth'kar's antennae hop to attention. "You know *kath*?"

She nods vigorously as she gathers up two menus. "It's made from insect protein. Very smart, actually. We Earthlings could learn something from you about sustainable farming and effective food distribution."

The hair on the back of my neck prickles while the hostess gazes at Roth'kar with adoring eyes. What is that about insect protein? How come she knows something about him I don't?

I want to say *hey, back off, he's mine*, but that would be ridiculous. Still, a nugget of fury seethes under the surface of my skin as the hostess finally does her job and leads us into the restaurant, toward a table for two. There's already a candle lit, and she gives each of us a menu before pulling out Roth'kar's chair, then gestures for him to sit there.

She does not pull out my chair.

"Thanks," I say in a clipped voice as the hostess opens her mouth once more to speak to Roth'kar. She seems to realize for the first time that I'm present, and with a bob of her head, quickly heads back to the host stand.

Roth'kar is holding the menu but watching my face as we're left alone. I try to school my expression into a smile now that we're seated and ready to eat, but my cheeks feel hot and my hands are clenched.

"Amara?" His brows lower in concern. "Was I... not supposed to speak with that woman?"

I don't even know what to make of his question. "Huh? What?"

"Well... it seems to have upset you. Is this an element of Earth culture I don't know? Should I not speak to other women?"

Oh, that's the last thing I want him to think. Now I feel like a major asshole for being possessive.

"No, no, not at all." I reach across to take his hand. "You can talk to anyone you like."

"That's good, because I would have had to confess that I talked to a woman the other day who made me a cooked brown tube in a bread bun. I did not ask for it, but she charged me five *bucks*."

I stare at him. "Cooked brown tube?"

"It tasted good." He hums thoughtfully. "It was dry, though."

Before I can go down the hole of wondering what sort of food he ate the other day, apparently given to him by a stranger, I shake my head.

"Wait, Roth'kar. What happened with the hostess, it was just... me being a brat." His antennae perk up, showing he's listening. "I thought she was hitting on you, and I didn't like the idea of someone hitting on you."

"She did not strike me," he says, puzzled.

"Flirting."

Roth'kar's translator works, then he nods. "I see."

"And I guess I feel a little, I don't know. Jealous, maybe? I don't want to share you with anyone else."

A faint smile tugs at his lips. "You felt jealous?"

"Well, she knew about the insect thing! I didn't know that. You eat insects?"

He chuckles. "Yes, the Karthinians eat insects, because they are easy to raise and then turn into *kath*."

"See?" I sigh. "She knew more about you than I do. And that makes me feel like a bad wife."

"You are anything but. In the short time I've been here, you have been a marvelous wife." He tilts his head. "It makes me happy that you felt protective of me."

We're interrupted by the waiter, who delivers our water and asks for drink orders. Roth'kar has no idea what the menu means, so I order for both of us, gambling on what I think he might like. He's not big into sweets but also doesn't enjoy bitter flavors. So I got him a Pisco Sour, thinking he would enjoy the texture of the foam.

We talk over the menu options, and I explain them as best I can, but Roth'kar has no idea about *pork loin in cherry sauce*—or what a cherry even is—which leaves it up to me. I order a few small plates so we can share and try out as many foods as possible, trying not to think too hard on the bill.

Tonight is about us, and enjoying ourselves, and hopefully... other things. Later.

Sexy lighting sounds nice right now.

CHAPTER FOURTEEN

ROTH'KAR

I AM IRRATIONALLY PLEASED at our encounter with the woman at the restaurant. I've never seen Amara go so stiff before, her full lips pressed together in a line, her dark eyes like knives. She has shown me mostly the happy, pleasant sides of herself, but not this side.

Not until tonight.

It excites me to see even more of her. She has claws hidden under her smiles, and I'm glad that she does so I don't have to worry about her when I'm not around. I like to know that she can protect herself. That she wants to protect *me*.

The drink that Amara ordered for me is lovely, far better than the *gin and tonic* I had when we went out to the club. It's refined, full of depth, and I spend a long time simply picking out each flavor and reading the ingredients off the menu. We can see out the windows from our table and gaze out over the vast city with its many twinkling lights. The Hole was a dark and decrepit place, with lighting to mark walkways—not bright neons and flashing shapes like this.

The human world is so *alive*.

And then the food arrives. Amara claps her hands together the way she always does, which I'm coming to enjoy about her, as it's spread out on the table. We serve ourselves, and Amara explains what each food item is as I add it to my plate. She sips her wine as I sip my cocktail, and we discuss each plate as we try it. There are so many wild and exotic flavors, all carefully built and layered. It's astounding, and nearly overwhelming, when there are four different dishes to choose from.

"Better than insects?" Amara asks, a playful glint in her eye.

"Far better." I taste another one of the little soft balls that Amara called *nyo-kee*. It's squishy in my mouth and utterly delicious. "*Kath* has one taste, and it is not a good one. Nothing compared to this."

When Amara is finished eating, I devour the rest. I'm not sure I'll be able to walk back to the bus stop.

"I hope they bring the check soon," Amara says, fiddling with her dress. Her wine is empty for the second time, and she keeps licking her lips, her eyes darting to mine and then away again. "I'd like to go."

I think I might know what's on her mind, and it's a problem I'm invested in solving so we can return home and be alone together. I glance around the restaurant for our waiter, then call out, "Hello, over here?"

Amara covers her face. "Oh my god, Roth'kar, you didn't."

The waiter comes over urgently. "What is it? Is your food all right?"

"Yes, we just need the..." I glance at Amara. "What was it, again? So we can leave?"

She spreads her fingers so she can look apologetically at the waiter. "The check, please."

He gives me an odd look that I can't decipher, then nods and leaves. When he's gone, Amara laughs.

"Next time, you wait patiently," Amara says. "You don't call them over."

"Why not?" That's a perplexing rule. "Then how do you tell them you want to go?"

"You don't. You wait."

"But..." I'm still confused. "Why?"

"I don't know!" Amara throws her hands into the air. "It's just how we do things. You know what, though, you're right. It's stupid." She laughs again, smiling at me so broadly it shows off her perfect white teeth. It's as if all the light in this room is focused on her.

Thankfully, the waiter returns with the *check*, and then we're off.

Amara leans on me while we wait with a few other humans for the bus.

"That was really nice," she says in a milky voice. I think she's feeling her wine. "Even when you yelled at the waiter."

"I raised my voice an appropriate amount."

She snorts, and it's adorable in its impropriety. "I

wonder what it would take for you to raise your voice an *inappropriate* amount?" She tilts her head and scoots toward me so she can kiss my neck. It's electrifying, sending a little bolt of pleasure right down my spine.

"I can imagine some activities."

Maybe I'm feeling my two cocktails, too.

Amara giggles, kissing my ear this time. "Oh, I'm imagining them."

I doubt she is imagining the truth, though. I learned from the Fact Sheet that the human version of my culans, the penis, is not similar in the least. What will Amara do when she's greeted with them? Will they frighten her?

Perhaps she will decide not to go forward with intimacy—or our marriage—after all.

That thought is unpleasant, and I try not to marinate on it as we finally get on the bus. We hop off only a few stops later. After it rumbles away, Amara tries to lead me off the street, into one of the darker pathways between buildings, but I come to a halt.

"We aren't supposed to leave the streetlights," I tell her, pulling her back. She blinks at me.

"Well, it's okay this time! It's just a shortcut. We got off at the wrong stop."

I look down the dark street and know that I can't let Amara walk down that way. This is my one job. To keep her safe.

"Streetlights only," I say, more firmly. "You told me those were the rules."

Amara scoffs, but then she pauses when she can tell I'm quite serious.

"Okaaay, fine, we'll just take the long way." She resumes trudging along the lighted sidewalk, and I'm relieved, even though she mutters something about *goody-two-shoes alien*.

We walk a good long way, and my head is clear again by the time we reach Amara's familiar apartment building. She is much less pleased, though, and keeps complaining that her feet hurt. Her shoes are not practical at all, but I don't mention this as we head inside.

In the apartment, Amara collapses on the couch. I lift her legs and sit down, setting them on my lap. Her feet are quite red in places, so I pick one up and rub it gently.

"Ooh." Amara's head falls back. "Oh yeah."

I think she likes this, so I decide to give her foot a good rub all over, trying to soothe out the aches and pains. She lets out noises that are even more erotic than those she makes when we kiss, and my culans lift their heads, wondering if she's ready for their services.

I gently push down on my crotch and adjust my jeans, then continue with her other foot.

"Damn, Roth'kar," Amara says, her eyes fluttering closed. "That's fucking great."

When I'm finished, she lies there flat and happy, a smile on her face. I lean over her and kiss her, and coyly, she kisses me back. Soon, I'm lying atop her, her legs spread open around my hips. I don't know quite how we got here, but I'm more than happy to kiss her more deeply, running my lower hands down to her thighs while my upper hands explore her ribcage.

I have been curious for quite some time about Amara's singular pair of breasts, and so, in a tentative and exploratory fashion, I stroke down the side of one. Amara presses into me like she wants more, so I venture upward, encircling it with my hand.

My culans leap to attention at the sensation of her breast's heavy weight in my palm. I run a finger up over the nipple, which is buried under fabric, and Amara's arms wind around my neck.

"This is nice," she says in my ear, "but I think it would be better if we had fewer clothes on."

Oh, *yes*. I wholly agree with this sentiment.

Perhaps I ought to attend to my own, but my hands are thirsting for Amara. I examine the buttons on her blouse, eventually figuring out how they work and then plucking them open one by one. She allows me to do it, watching with interest until the shirt falls free of her shoulders, revealing yet more fabric underneath that holds her breasts in place.

They are larger than I expected, more voluptuous now that I see them without her clothes on. She reaches behind her back and fiddles with something, and then that fabric drops away, too.

Oh, is she beautiful, with two teardrop breasts and fat, brown areolas. My culans have fully swollen, clasping each other as I run two hands up her ribcage to those twin swells, getting a sense of them, the shape and size, the soft texture of the flesh and the darker skin of the nipple. I read in the Fact Sheet that much like Karthinians with breasts, these are also used to feed young—and behave as erogenous zones.

While still holding onto her hips, I flick a thumb over her nipple, and Amara responds with a gasp, so I do it on the other breast, too. She reaches out and drags my mouth down to hers as I touch her, so we can do the making out at the same time.

Growing bolder, I squeeze her nipples and then soothe

them, rubbing them with my palms. But now I want to lick them the way I'm licking her mouth, so I do, stroking her cheek before I dive down to suck them.

Amara arches her back when I do this, so I tug harder, tonguing the nipple and then releasing it before repeating with the other breast.

"Now you," she manages between gasps. "Take off your shirt, Roth'kar."

I comply right away, leaning back so I can shuck the shirt off onto the floor. Amara's eyes take me in, roaming from my hip up to my shoulders, and then to my eyes. That broad smile I find so beautiful shines up at me.

"Damn, you're a smokeshow." As usual, I don't know what it is, but by the way she says it while licking her lips, I think I have an idea. She strokes my upper arms, then slides her touch inward toward my belly button. She moves farther down, to the point at which the taper of my muscle disappears into my jeans. "What about these?"

Now is the moment. Perhaps I should prepare her for what she's about to see.

"You know that I am…" I clear my throat, not sure how to introduce this subject. "Different, yes?"

She cocks her head. "I mean, no offense, but you are an alien."

I nod agreeably. "And we are sexually compatible," I remind her. "But it may not look like what you're accustomed to."

"Okay, now you're freaking me out." Amara chuckles nervously. "What is it? I have to see."

I reach for the button of the jeans, hoping that she does not change her mind. Once I take them off, my culans are pushing eagerly at the confines of my human underwear—a mystifying additional layer of clothing. Amara watches raptly as I hook a finger in the band and pull them down, letting myself free.

She gasps sharply and covers her mouth as they appear. I try to keep my own anxiety at bay as my culans clasp together, the soft teeth intertwined.

"Holy shit," Amara says, her eyes huge. "You weren't kidding."

CHAPTER FIFTEEN

AMARA

AT FIRST, it's hard to tell what I'm looking at. Roth'kar certainly does not have a human penis, I can say that much. It appears to be more like two penises clasped together with ridges, where the ridges interlock to form a single shaft. When Roth'kar inhales a deep breath, they suddenly part, revealing that they are, in fact, two halves of a single whole. They curl back like a maw opening, waving in the air before they close and lock together again.

I have never, ever seen anything like it. It is distinctly alien, distinctly strange—and utterly compelling. How does it work? What would it feel like?

"Do you want to stop?" Roth'kar asks, his cheeks now an even darker, ruddier purple. "If you are not ready—"

"No, no." I wave my hands. "It's okay. I'm just surprised. You're right, it's very different."

The alien penis is definitely erect, and as the two

halves squeeze together, the tines along the edges protrude. Those can't possibly be sharp—they look soft and rounded, and I wonder what texture they are.

"Can I touch it?" I ask, peering up into Roth'kar's blue eyes. He's staring back at me, his expression the picture of discomfort.

"S-sure. If you want to."

I have no idea what to expect as I stroke the left side with just two fingers, testing the surface. It's soft, with loose skin that moves up and down much like a foreskin. The two halves part at my touch and curl toward me, seeking more. I trace a finger over the ridges that run along the edge of each one, and they're perfectly pliable, soft to the touch and made of flesh like the rest of him.

A shiver ripples through me, wondering what they would feel like.

Roth'kar grips the back of the couch as the two halves come together again. With care and gentleness, I wrap my hand around both, squeezing ever so slightly, and he groans.

"Is that... good?" I stroke up and then down again. The ridges extend outward under my hand, creating a bumpy texture.

"Oh yes," Roth'kar answers quickly. "That's wonderful."

I notice at the tips of each half are slits—dual urethras, how interesting—and pre-cum is already gathering there. I wonder what sort of anatomy a female Karthinian has.

And I wonder if Karthinians enjoy blowjobs, too.

I lick my lips as I stroke him a hair faster, letting my hand drag from the tapered heads all the way down to the root. Underneath hangs a pair of surprisingly human-looking balls, but lacking any hair there the way a human would have. In fact, his whole crotch is hairless, and it's yet another interesting difference between us.

Roth'kar's head drifts back, his spine arching as I really get into the rhythm. Two of his hands are curled into fists, while the other two grab onto whatever they can.

"Roth'kar," I murmur, getting his attention. I lean forward, changing my position on the couch so I'm on my knees in front of him.

"Mm, yes?"

"Can I put my mouth on you?"

His eyebrows rise high on his forehead. "Your mouth? On my culans?"

"Is that what they're called?"

"Y-yes." He's watching me carefully. "Do whatever you like."

Emboldened, I lower my head and lick the tip of one side. It spasms, so I repeat the motion with the other one, earning the same reaction. I resume stroking, but only at the base as I ease the tapered tip between my lips.

When I bring him into my mouth, Roth'kar lets out an unguarded groan.

"*Shavek*," he mutters, which must be a Karthinian word that doesn't translate. Perhaps a curse or a prayer. "That is incredible."

I've barely begun. Thinking wicked thoughts, I keep him shallow for a few moments, sucking and circling with my tongue. Then, as he shivers under me, I sink his culans deep into my throat. I take it as far as I can, and I'm rewarded by Roth'kar's hips bucking up off the couch. The ridges tickle as I swallow them up, then hollow my cheeks and suck as I pull him back out again.

"Oh, Amara." When I look up, his culans still buried in my mouth, my alien is staring down at me with huge, black pupils. "That is exquisite. Is this... also kissing?"

I almost choke on his alien dick. Carefully, I slide him out from between my lips.

"This, my friend, is a blowjob."

His culans flex in my hands, those soft teeth extending and shuddering.

"It is an incredible thing," Roth'kar says, almost reverently. "This *blowjob*."

"Do you not do this back home?"

"No. It is..." He tries to find the right words. "Ah, intercourse is perfunctory. It is not a dance, a tease, as this is."

I think I understand. He's never had a lot of foreplay and just dove right into the thick of things before.

"It's an exploration, too," I offer, still stroking him with a gentle, measured evenness. "A way for us to get to know each other better." Already, spending all this time with his bizarre, wonderful cock has made me... thirsty. I have a craving between my thighs, imagining this inside me. What would it feel like when those two halves separated? What could they do?

"I would be getting to know you better if you weren't wearing so many clothes," Roth'kar says, a little hint of a smirk on his face.

"Then let me fix that." I release him, and the two culans separate, waving in the air while I reach for the zipper on my skirt. Then I pull it down, and while I'm at it, I toss away my underwear, too.

Roth'kar's gaze is pinned on me. "Now I would like to be the one to explore."

I lean back on the couch arm as he crawls toward me. He takes my ankles in his lower hands, the upper ones roaming upward, to my calf and over my knee, then to my thighs. It's amazing how he can be in so many places at once.

"I read about humans, as much as I could," Roth'kar says, running his thumbs over the inside of my thigh. "But none of it compares to seeing you."

I trimmed down my bush recently, wondering if we might get to this point, but I didn't shave anything. Maybe I should have, knowing that Karthinians don't have hair there like we do.

But, if anything, Roth'kar seems to find it interesting, skating one palm over my flank to the curly hair at the crux of my legs. He tangles his finger in it, studying it. Then he lowers that finger, trailing it down one of the lips of my pussy.

"Ah, there it is," he says, and I wonder what he's talking about for only a split second before he touches my clit. It's a burst of sensation, wonderful and welcome. Roth'kar tilts his head. "The Fact Sheet was not incorrect about the clitoris, it seems." He touches me a few more times experimentally.

Fact Sheet? I wish I'd gotten one of those.

"Try rubbing it," I tell him, already growing desperate for more. So he does, keeping the pressure light, his eyes on my face as I gasp and shiver. It's one thing to touch yourself, as I have been doing for the last few years, and another thing when it's someone else.

"I need lubrication," Roth'kar mutters. He looks down at his own groin, then whisks the tip of his finger through the pre-cum he's been dripping for some time now. When he rubs me again, it's wetter, and he glides back and forth like a dream.

Wow. That was exceedingly hot.

One of his lower hands drops to his culans, wrapping around them while he teases me. That's really hot, too—that he can hold my ass in place, touch my clit, and touch himself at the same time.

Fuck, and he's so *good* at it. He varies his patterns and pressure, winding me up and then dragging it out, until I'm jerking against his hand and craving something inside me.

"Tell me what to do," Roth'kar says in a quiet voice, leaning over me. "Tell me how best to please you. Can I give you the blowjob? As you did for me?"

Oh, he wants to eat me out? Fuck yes.

"Please," I manage while he continues his circuit. "Yes, do that. But first..." I take his hand in mine, and he stops his attack on my clit, allowing me to guide him lower. I watch his face as his finger slips between my folds, reaching the wetness inside.

Roth'kar nods in understanding, and carefully explores, sifting through the layers until he reaches my entrance. There, he pushes his finger in, and it slides gloriously into me.

"Yes, like that," I praise him, and his antennae perk up.

"Shall I blowjob you and do this at the same time?"

I nod feverishly. I like the soft, shy smile that crosses his face as he crouches down between my legs, his sculpted ass in the air, and brushes his tongue over my clit.

"Oh, damn," I moan. He slides that finger in deeper, and his mouth absolutely goes to town. He licks, sucks, kisses, caresses—all the words in the dictionary for whatever his tongue and lips are doing. Once his hand is buried in me as far as it can go, he withdraws, still keeping his touch gentle, and then pushes it in again.

And fuck, it's so good that I'm shaking, and my pleasure is a living thing snaking up my spine.

"Use two of them," I manage to whimper. I need more, so much more.

Immediately, there's a second finger there, and I'm so wet that it slides in easily. Now that he's using both of them, his rhythm speeds up as my moans rise in volume. God, he's so good at this I might just blow up into a million pieces.

"Amara," Roth'kar says, and I glance down to see him observing me over my pubic hair, his mouth wet. "You are delicious."

A shiver runs along my spine as he ducks his head down again to devour me. I'm clutching his hair, keening as he pumps his fingers faster, his tongue flicking my clit every which way until all my muscles tighten and sparks fly behind my closed eyelids.

And then I crack. It's like a pot boiling over as my orgasm races through me, an acute, powerful bliss unlike anything I can achieve with just my vibrator.

Slowly, Roth'kar withdraws his hand and smooths it over my hypersensitive clit. He crouches over me, his lower hand urgently stroking his culans. "I do not want to rush you, but I would very much like to—"

"Fuck me," I demand, reaching to cover his hands with mine. He releases himself, letting me run my palms up and down his cock—or that's what I'm calling it, anyway.

"Fuck...?" He squints at me. "A curse word. The translator does not want to elaborate."

Despite the intimacy of this moment, I have to laugh.

"It means have sex with me. But do it fast and hard."

His eyes widen significantly. Then, nodding, Roth'kar lifts my thighs and positions himself between them. I watch with curiosity as his culans part, and one of them strokes over my clit, which makes my body riot again. The other one brushes downward, through the lips of my pussy and over my entrance.

This is as wonderful as it is insane. Yes, I am going to have sex with my new alien husband and his toothy tentacle penis. And why shouldn't I? I'm a woman with her own job and her own condo in 2029. I can do what I want.

Roth'kar wraps his fist around the base of his cock, and the culans obediently come back together, their tines interlocking once more until they're a smooth shaft with ridges along the sides. I watch with amazement as the tapered tip slips through my folds, and easily, my pussy opens for it.

While still gripping himself with his lower hands, Roth'kar reaches up with the higher pair and flicks my nipples, and it's incredible his brain can be in both places at once.

Then more of him pushes through, and now those softened ridges are making themselves known. And holy fuck, does it feel like nothing else on this earth. I gasp as it widens me, pushing into me. Roth'kar grunts, releasing himself as he sinks in deeper. Oh, those two tentacled things are not small, either, and the stretch sends shockwaves through me.

"You are so wet," he says, biting his lip as he pauses his descent, then pulls himself back. "And so tight around me." Soft teeth once again drag over the inside of me, and I can't help the cry that escapes.

My voice comes out as a whimper. "And you feel absolutely amazing."

I finally look up, as fascinated as I've been with the sight of him sliding inside me. Roth'kar's blue eyes are even brighter than before, and he lowers his head toward mine as he thrusts deeper. And that texture, I can barely stand it as every movement of his hips drags those delightful tines in and out.

"My culans have ached for you, Amara," he says, lowering his body on top of mine, his second set of hands gripping my hips while his upper one cradles my cheek. "They have longed only to please you."

"They are pleasing me—" I moan as Roth'kar reaches a new depth inside me. "—immensely."

"Good." He nips at my lips, and when they open, he fucks me with his mouth, too, his tongue lashing mine while he maintains a steady, even rhythm.

That's when I feel it. The culans are separating inside me, spreading open, pushing me wider as Roth'kar continues pumping his hips. Now the stretch feels almost impossible, and I let out a strangled cry. Those tines are brushing over something wonderful inside me, and my whole body spasms with each of his thrusts. Usually, the few times I've slept with men, it takes me eons to get there with just vaginal sex—but right now, I'm standing in the shadow of an immense climax, and with every intentional movement, Roth'kar is driving it closer and closer.

"Ah! Please!" I sob, though I'm not sure what I'm

asking for. But he takes it as an invitation to fuck me faster, harder, and I'm clinging onto him so tight I wonder if I'm hurting him. My legs are wrapped around his waist, heels digging into his lower back, as that shadow over me grows taller and taller.

"Yes, Amara. My beautiful human." Roth'kar looks into my eyes, and the endless blue of them threatens to swallow me up. He is beautiful, too. "Give it all to me. Come apart."

So I do. I break into pieces in his arms, a full-throated scream escaping from my throat as the shadow crashes down, and then the sheer, crushing bliss steals my breath. Roth'kar lets out a guttural groan, slamming into me again and again. His culans fill me up even more, and I'm squeezing down so hard I might just burst into nothing.

When he unleashes, Roth'kar's eyes roll back and something hot and wet gushes inside me. He shudders all over, his lower hands digging into my flesh. Another shudder travels through both of us as I clench around him, our pleasure a shared being between us.

Roth'kar drops onto two elbows so our bodies are flush, and I can see my own satisfaction reflected in his eyes.

Wow. I just got railed by an alien, and it might have been the best thing to ever happen to me.

CHAPTER SIXTEEN

ROTH'KAR

IT WAS a fascinating experience to do that with a human, especially with Amara. Karthinian females have a single vagina with two channels departing from it, and the culans are designed to fill both at the same time. Having them pressed tightly together inside Amara's singular passage was like no feeling I've ever experienced. My pleasure was so profound I struggled immensely just to wait until she had reached her conclusion, and then her glorious scream pulled me over the edge of my control. By then, my culans were writhing inside her, and I hope that did not feel too strange.

I don't think it did, though, by the look of sheer carnal bliss on Amara's face. Her lashes swing low over her eyes as she runs one of her hands through my hair.

"Wow," she murmurs, kissing the tip of my nose in a way that's both adorable and delicate. "That was incredible."

I remain seated in her as my culans twine back together, and the blood slowly drains out of them.

"As it was for me, as well." I let my belly press down into hers, holding up my chest on my elbows. My lower hands smooth down her sides, just reveling in her soft swells. "I hope I get to do it many more times."

Amara giggles, her cheeks dark and her eyes alight. "Yes, please. In many more ways, too."

I am curious what other ways she has in mind.

"Roth'kar."

I stroke her cheek, pushing some of her long, dark hair aside. "Yes?"

She looks at me shyly, then away again. "Do you want to, um, sleep in my bed with me?"

It's so gingerly spoken that I smile down at her. This human is so eager and yet so tentative, carefully peeling back the layers of her heart for me.

"Yes." I kiss her lips, my fingers wandering down to cup her chin. "I would enjoy this very much."

At last, I withdraw from her, my culans now limp, and my spend spills out deliciously. Amara lets out a delightful little moan as I sit back, surveying my handiwork. She's sprawled naked across the couch, and I fetch a towel from the kitchen and wet it in the sink. As I clean her up, I can't believe she let me inside her, that she was willing to accept me.

I take Amara's hand and lift her to her feet, then, still holding onto her, lead her back to the bedroom. She sighs with contentment when she flops down on the bed, and then she pulls me down next to her.

And *shavek*, is this bed soft. It's not at all like the futon in my room, but lush and giving under my body, conforming to my shape. I can't help a groan of pleasure as I lean back on the pillow.

"Memory foam," she says in my ear, slinging one arm over my chest. "I think you'll like it."

Eventually we find our way under the blankets, and Amara flips off the light. In the darkness, she curls up at my side, and I bring her in even closer with my arms.

"That was really fucking great," she whispers to me.

I have to smile. "As it was for me, too."

"Good." Amara strokes my bare chest a few times before her hand slowly stops, and her breath evens out. It's rather easy to drift off with her, sleeping on a cloud.

I'm awoken by the sound of a blaring noise. Amara groans next to me, then reaches for the bedside table and smacks some object there. The noise ceases immediately, but by then I'm already sitting up in bed, wondering if our ship is about to crash.

"Sorry," she mumbles, sitting up. "That stupid thing is the only reason I can get up in the morning." She yawns and stretches, then slides out of bed to put on her clothes. I do the same, now that my things are in her drawers, and we emerge ready for the day.

Quickly Amara throws together breakfast, then heads off to work. Once again, I have the day to myself—something which is no longer as novel as it once was.

So to keep myself busy, I clean. I scrub the counters, even the walls behind them, which have splashes of red sauce on them. I climb up on Amara's step stool to reach the high corners of the living room, where some kind of white string has accrued.

I nearly fall off it when a tiny animal with eight legs drops onto my hand. I have no idea what sort of creature it is, but reflexively, I toss it away. It lands on the ground easily and runs, vanishing behind the television.

Gross. I consider looking for it and crushing it, but I don't know if I ever want to see it again.

I'll have to ask Amara about that. She probably does not want tiny eight-legged creatures living in her condo.

Then I move on to the bedroom, making the bed, organizing our belongings in the dresser, rearranging my clothes in the closet. I don't dare to touch Amara's in case she has them in some type of order, but I pick up clothing that has fallen on the floor and straighten all her shoes, most of which look like the kind that hurt her feet.

What an odd choice. But the shoes did make her butt look very nice.

When I'm done, I clean up the room that was formerly mine, taking all the bedding off the futon now that I won't be using it. I fold and pile it up, then clean the corners and walls of this room, too.

When I'm finished, it's only early afternoon, so I head out of the apartment to walk to the park. I'm used to the stares I get. Today, a small Earthling child with thick black curls breaks away from her mother and runs toward me.

"Alien!" She stops in front of me as her mother chases her. "Wow! So cool. What are you?"

I crouch so I can get a better look at her. "I am Karthinian."

"So sorry," the woman says, grabbing the little girl's hand. "Izzy's only four."

"It's all right." I smile at the two of them, as I have not had the chance to interact with a human child yet. "You are new to me, too."

The girl cocks her head. "You have so many arms."

"I do. I can carry many bags of groceries."

The mother barks a laugh. "I bet someone in your life finds that very useful."

They are on a walk, and so the mother, Sylvia, invites me to walk with them so her child can ask me more questions. Izzy is very eager to learn all about *New Dro'thar II*, and I try to spin a tale that is much less sordid than reality.

"I am glad I came to Earth, though," I tell them. "Your sun is beautiful, and I have a very lovely wife."

Sylvia, who has bountiful curls like her daughter, beams at me. "I thought you might be with the Matching Program. I'm sure she's a lucky lady."

"I know that I am a lucky Karthinian male."

When we reach the end of the path, we say goodbye, and I walk the rest of the way home much lighter on my feet. But when I reach the condo, my communicator chirps.

Who could be trying to reach me? For a moment, I worry that it's Gazargo, the little alien matchmaker, calling to tell me that I must go home. But surely that isn't it.

When I answer, my communicator displays a hologram of someone familiar. It is my friend Zono once again.

"Ah, Roth'kar!" he says when I accept the call. "It's good to see you."

I cannot say the same. Seeing Zono inside his room, the walls dark and dirty, the ceiling leaking, takes me back to a place in my mind that I rather would not be. I am grateful to see a familiar face, of course, but it also reminds me of what I chose to leave behind.

"Hello," I say, instead of returning the greeting. "I didn't expect your call."

"You thought I wouldn't check in on you?" Zono gives a grudging laugh. "You were wrong, friend. We all talk about you, you know. How you escaped the Hole." He clucks as he studies me. "Shiny new clean clothes, I see. The new 'wife' must be caring for you well."

He makes it sound as if I am a kept pet, like one of those four-legged *dogs*.

"She did buy these, yes." I keep the indignation out of my voice. "She is a kind and responsible woman."

Zono cocks a brow. "Ooh. So you like her? I didn't think that was part of your plan."

It pains me when he utters these words, this reminder of how I came into this marriage. I did not yet know Amara, and now that I do, I'm certain it would hurt her to learn this.

"Plans change," I mutter.

"I like to hear this." Zono wears a sincere smile. "I'm glad that you are finding happiness there."

I suppose I am, one day at a time. Especially after last night, knowing that more nights like that lie ahead of me buoys me.

"I would do anything, as you did, to have clothes like yours and some fresh food to eat. You've already gained weight."

I suppose I have, and it's not unwelcome. I have been

doing some exercises to stay healthy, and now I have the nutrition to fuel my body.

"Amara will be home soon," I say, because it makes me too guilty to continue this conversation. "I ought to go."

Disappointment crosses his face. "All right. Perhaps one of her friends might apply to the Program."

I don't dissuade him from his belief, and then we end the call.

Even after I've put the communicator away, though, guilt gnaws at me. Speaking to Zono today made me realize just how callous I was with Amara's feelings coming into this, and that wasn't right, not with such a tender person as she is.

I'm overwhelmed with relief when she finally returns home, singing, "It's Friday! It's Friday!" as she swoops in the door. I catch her, and Amara wraps her arms lovingly around my neck, kissing me on each cheek.

"Good to see you, handsome," she says in a sultry tone. "Shall we go out tonight? My coworker Kendall invited us."

Another evening dancing and drinking and spending time with Amara? I would never say no.

"I look forward to meeting her." I head into the bedroom to change. "What color should I wear?"

Amara's eyes light up. "Oh my god, can we match? That would be so cute."

"If you would like."

"Oh, I would *like*." She giggles as she follows me through the doorway. I can't help grabbing her again, imagining throwing her down on that bed and kissing her thoroughly.

"We don't have to be there until eight," Amara says, her eyes following mine. "Want to take off my work clothes before we put the nice ones on?"

"Absolutely." I'm already peeling off my shirt. "I want to try these *other ways* you spoke of."

CHAPTER SEVENTEEN

AMARA

MY NEXT SEXY lesson with Roth'kar is about doggie style. He warms me up in missionary, then I flip over and spread my legs for him. When I glance over my shoulder, his mouth is hanging open, almost comically. Then he swallows and approaches, his culans snapping closed as he readies himself.

He feels even more incredible at this angle, in this position. I might just combust. Roth'kar really gets into it, growling my name and reaching around me with his many arms to tweak my nipples, stroke my clit, touch me everywhere.

I come so hard I see stars.

When we're finished, he pulls me into his arms.

"I liked that position," he says. "This *doggie style.* Despite the name."

I waggle my eyebrows. "Wait until you see cowgirl."

After a while of cuddling, Roth'kar says, "We ought to

get ready." He helps me up off the bed, but I got fucked so senseless I'm a little wobbly on my legs. "Think you can dance tonight?"

"Psh." I flap a hand at him. "I can always dance."

When I've recovered my senses, we make a quick dinner out of some leftovers, then head for the bus stop.

"We're going to meet Kendall," I tell him as we find our seats. "She's my work bestie. There's no better way to bond than in the trenches of an office."

Roth'kar nods sagely, like he understands. "No friends like friends on sewer duty."

Kendall is meeting us at Skunk, a big venue downtown where her favorite DJ is playing. The place can fit three or four hundred people, and Rooster Squad is popular, so I expect a wild night ahead of us.

"I'm already in line," Kendall texts me when we arrive. "Come sneak in."

We get some dirty looks as we slide in behind Kendall, but most people are too surprised by the blue alien in their midst to be upset about it.

"So here he is, in the flesh," Kendall says, spreading her arms wide when she greets Roth'kar. He stares at her, clearly not knowing what she's about to do. She hugs him with a bear hug, the way she does everyone, and his arms flatten against his sides.

Kendall guffaws. "Aliens don't do a lot of hugging, huh?"

Roth'kar shakes his head, eyes wide. "Not typically with strangers."

"I'm not a stranger!" She places her hands on her hips. "You're Amara's beau, which means you're my friend now. Sorry!"

She trounces ahead of us, her ticket held out as we approach the counter. I buy tickets for Roth'kar and me, and then we're inside, the walls already rattling. Huge speakers line the stage, the kind that I know better than to stand too near. That's how you get tinnitus, thank you.

Kendall leads us to the bar, where we have to wait in line again before we're served. We order gin and tonics, and then head upstairs to the second level, where we can look out over the railing at all the people going wild down below.

"This place is cool, huh, Roth'kar?" Kendall asks, sipping her drink. "My favorite venue. And Rooster Squad is awesome. This is going to be a great show."

As the opener finally finishes and their equipment is cleared away, a tall woman in a huge rooster head comes out on stage. The crowd goes absolutely ballistic as she bows, then lowers her hands to the turntables.

I don't remember much after that. We finish our drinks and head down the stairs again, getting sucked into the whorl of dancers taking up the main floor. When we're exhausted from dancing to the frenetic pace of the music, we go for more drinks and slug them down fast. Kendall finds someone to dance with on our second foray, and she waves at me as she's whisked away. Now Roth'kar's arms are around my waist, and he's smoothing them down my hips as we start to move in time with the beat.

We have more drinks, and then return to the dance floor, swerving and shaking our bodies faster and faster. Time disappears, and all there is before me is my alien, his bright blue eyes boring into mine before he leans down to kiss me. We kiss and dance at the same time, his cock thickening under his pants as we gyrate our hips together.

A few other dancers hoot and holler at us, and Roth'kar's antennae shrink in embarrassment, but he kisses me anyway.

How we get home is a mystery, but we manage, stumbling in the front door of my condo and laughing after Roth'kar told me his story about the surprise spider.

"Spiders aren't *bad*, per se," I tell him. "Some of them are, like, super dangerous. But not most."

"*Some* of them?"

"The ones who are good just, like, eat mosquitos and leave us alone."

He does not look convinced by my argument in favor of spiders.

"It was tiny," he says, very seriously. "The tiny ones are the ones you must watch out for."

I can't help laughing, and he seems offended by this, so I kiss him all over, even his antennae. He moans when I do this, and I feel like a dumbass for not having tried touching him here before.

"Very sensitive," Roth'kar warns as I straddle him on the couch, kissing his ear and stroking one of them.

"I'll be careful, then."

Soon he's good and hard for me, and even though we just had sex a few hours ago, I'm already in dire need of having him inside me. So I strip off his jeans, then pull up my skirt and dispense of my underwear before sitting on him again.

His culans part, one of them sliding up and over my clit, the other downward, over my sex and toward my ass. Roth'kar cocks his head.

"You know," he says thoughtfully, "there are two of them."

I know immediately what he's implying, and I'm all about it.

"Fuck me hard right now," I tell him, kissing the tip of his nose, "and then yes. I want to do that, too."

For the first time that I've ever seen, Roth'kar gets a wicked smile on his face. His culans clasp together, and then he guides himself inside me, right where he belongs.

"Fuck," I say, sagging forward as he glides into his seat right away. "That's so incredible."

"You are incredible, Amara." Two of his hands lift me by my ass, then lower me down again. I moan as he burrows into me a second time. "I am so, so lucky I was matched with you."

We fuck that way until my legs give out, and then Roth'kar throws me unceremoniously onto the couch on my stomach, my ass in the air. Then he really goes to town, and those amazing soft ridges drive me wild again. I come hard, but Roth'kar doesn't. He just keeps going, clasping me with all of his hands, reaching down around my thigh and between my legs to play with my clit.

Soon, I can't take any more, and he finally lets go. I collapse to the couch, and he nearly falls down on top of me.

"Sorry," he says into my hair. "It was really hard to orgasm."

I snort into the fabric cushion. "That'll be the alcohol. Not that I'm complaining."

Then, finally, we're in bed—and I'm not sure how I got there, either. I fall asleep to Roth'kar stroking my hair, saying, "There are no good spiders."

The next morning, of course, we both pay for it.

Neither of us has the energy to cook, so we drag ourselves a few blocks down to a cheap diner that serves bitter coffee and massive pancakes. I load up on grease and sugar, then suck down coffee. Roth'kar tries it a second time, and though he squints like it tastes bad, he has a few more sips, squinting like it hurts and heals at the same time.

Then we're back at the apartment, napping in front of a movie. I might be hungover, but I'm pleased as a cat, curled up with Roth'kar and snacking on caramel popcorn.

I might just be happy.

Time flies by. Roth'kar expresses interest in getting out of the house more and having things he can do while I'm at work. Because even though we spend all of my time at home together, I'm also gone for eight hours a day on weekdays, which is a lot of time for him to spend alone.

He inquires about working at the corner store, but until he has permanent citizenship on Earth, he can't take a job. Still, now he knows it's a possibility, and that seems to excite him for the future. He goes to the park every day, where he has befriended a mother and daughter who play on the playground. The daughter is fascinated with him, and he likes to entertain her curiosity, answering questions about Karthinian life and culture.

It feels inevitable now that Roth'kar will stay. I spent so much time wondering if he might choose to leave at the end of this, but these days, I'm almost sure what he'll choose. He doesn't need to tell me in so many words, but he's happier now than when he first arrived. He smiles more, and eventually, opens up about his life on the spaceship. I don't know how he survived it, and I start to understand better why he's been reluctant to tell me about that time.

The Hole sounds like a terrible place. He tries to pepper his descriptions with good things, like the sense of community they shared, but I can tell that it's still painful to think back on. I remind him that he's here now, with me, and we have each other.

As we approach the end of the trial, any anxiety I might have had about us as a couple fades. We both sought a partner in life, someone we could love, and we found it. I have to hand it to Gazargo for making it possible.

It's almost Halloween, and Roth'kar has enjoyed the sight of pumpkins popping up on porches all around the neighborhood, people stringing up decorations in their windows and skeletons in their yards.

"Are those... bloody handprints?" Roth'kar asks, mouth twisting as we pass some windows smeared with blood. "Like in that movie we saw?"

"Oh yeah. Cool, huh?"

We've been watching some horror movies to get into the Halloween mood, and Roth'kar is riveted by them. He clings to me during the scary scenes, and once I even catch him hiding his face with a hand, peeking out between his fingers. After the first scary movie, he was so rattled that I was certain he'd never want to watch one again.

But he did the very next night. And the night after that.

He expresses an interest in decorating the condo, so we pick up some spiderwebbing and hang a few bats in front. Roth'kar is immensely pleased by the act of picking out where each bat will go, and even cajoles me into buying some of those same bloody handprints for the big window.

"They will believe someone has been murdered in your house," he says gleefully. "But the trick is that no one has been murdered!"

Then I suggest we visit a haunted house, the very same thing he had once thought to be a ridiculous activity. But if anything, he's excited by the prospect, and so we get tickets to a big one outside of town. There's a corn maze involved and a barn full of butcher implements. We're both absolutely scared out of our skins when a man leaps out with a chainsaw, but we run away giggling, arm in arm.

Soon, it's going to be time for the biggest, best party of the year—the one Marguerite holds at her house. All our friends will be there, as will dozens of other strangers. Marguerite knows everyone and has whole other friend groups I've never even met.

"We need costumes," I tell Roth'kar a few days before the party.

He's familiar now with the concept, having seen a man dressed like a chicken trying to sell fried chicken.

"Do I need one?" Roth'kar asks, holding up his four arms and waggling his antennae. I laugh outright.

"It's about the spirit of the thing, but no, you really don't have to."

"I will. For you." And then he kisses me, and I forget whatever we were just talking about.

CHAPTER EIGHTEEN

ROTH'KAR

I HAVE CHOSEN to be a cat for Halloween. It is the mortal enemy of a dog, or so they tell me, making it the natural choice. This involves a pair of cat ears on a band over my head, and some makeup that gives me a pink nose and black whiskers, and black clothing. It's simple, but effective, vaguely resembling the picture Amara showed me.

On the other hand, my wife goes "all out," as her friend Kendall says. We head downtown to find Amara's perfect costume. She considers dressing as a Karthinian so we could be a pair, but I remind her I will be a cat, not a Karthinian, and she laughs one of her amazing, uproarious laughs.

Eventually she finds the perfect red sequin dress, deciding to go as a character from a movie we watched, *Moulin Rouge*. Her body looks flawless in it, and I am tempted to rip it off her when she emerges from the fitting room.

Then, it's the night of the party, and a cool rain is coming down. I didn't know water could fall from the sky, and I spend far too long standing in it, reveling in the feeling of it landing on my face before Amara hands me an umbrella.

"You'll ruin your makeup!" she says as she shows me how to open it. The umbrella pops up to cover my head, and I think it's a rather genius invention.

We get on a new kind of bus—a light rail, Amara calls it—that moves much faster and smoother. It zooms along, the lights of the city flickering through the big windows. We fly past immensely tall buildings until we're clear on the other side. Then trees take over the landscape, and I'm still amazed at them, how luscious they are even as the leaves start to change color.

It is, perhaps, the most beautiful thing I've ever seen, aside from my wife.

Finally, the light rail comes to a stop and Amara gets up.

"This is us!" she says, grabbing my hand, and we hop off together. We pull out our umbrellas again and head off down the street, hand in hand.

It's not long before we reach a rather large home with all the lights on and dozens of vehicles parked outside. The noise coming from the interior is so loud that it's audible even as we approach.

"Fashionably late," Amara says proudly as we go up the steps to the front door. She doesn't even knock, as she had taught me to do, before opening it.

We're greeted by a burst of noise—people talking and

laughing, music booming. The house appears to be filled to the brim with humans dressed in costume and carrying red plastic cups.

"Amara!" someone calls out, and Fiona emerges from the crowd, throwing herself at Amara. After they've hugged, Fiona turns to me, and I think fast enough to open my arms to her before she hugs me, too.

"Show us to the drinks?" Amara asks.

Fiona leads the way into the kitchen, where we find Marguerite standing in front of a huge bowl of pink liquid, smoke rising off the top and billowing out onto the floor. She scoops some of the liquid and ladles it into a cup, one for me and one for Amara.

I sniff it suspiciously.

"Extremely alcoholic punch," Marguerite explains. "Be careful."

It's sweet and sour on my tongue, and I know immediately why it comes with a caution. It would be much too easy to drink a lot of it, and fast.

Once we have our beverages, we say goodbye to Marguerite and follow Fiona into the living room, which is packed with people in various states of dress. I find another cat, but she has almost no clothes on, which seems odd when she is supposedly dressing as a furred animal.

We dance and drink, then when we're too hot, we head outside onto the covered porch to enjoy the sound of rain. It comes with a lovely, strange smell, too, that I breathe in deeply as we step outside. A few others have already gathered out here and stand in an odd circle.

"Oooh," Amara says, sniffing the air. "Someone brought the goodies."

"Goodies?" I ask.

She gives me a huge, mischievous grin. "Want to try something new?"

I glance down at my drink, then up at her again. She hasn't led me wrong yet when it comes to trying new things, so I might as well.

"Sure."

Amara taps on someone's shoulder, and the circle opens for us. There are a few gasps as I step into the ring.

"Oh, dang, an alien!" says one man dressed in an elaborate suit and top hat. He is one of the few human males I've seen since coming to Earth. "I haven't met an alien before. How are you, man?"

I blink. "I am not a man."

"Indeed!" He laughs a surprisingly loud, boisterous laugh. "Are you two joining us?"

"Yes, please," says Amara, and someone hands her two small objects. She lifts a glass tube with a bowl at the end to her lips, then flicks the little cylinder and a burst of flame comes out. She brings the flame down to the bowl and inhales the smoke into her mouth. After holding it for a moment, she releases the smoke, then hands me the glass object.

"Put the pipe to your lips and breathe in."

I do as she tells me, and she brings the flame down to the bowl again. I inhale, and the smoke invading my throat nearly makes me gag.

"Bring it into your lungs," Amara instructs, and though it's uncomfortable, I do it. She takes the pipe from me as the smoke fills my diaphragm, and then I cough, sending it all back out.

It tastes awful, and the sensation of smoke in my lungs

is unnatural. The pipe travels around the circle as everyone resumes talking.

"Did you know that what we think of as the 'angler-fish' is just a female, and the males are really tiny?" the man in the top hat says. "After they impregnate the females, they get *absorbed into her body*."

Everyone lets out *oohs* and *ahhs*.

"So basically, they're just sperm donors and then they get eaten?" Amara asks.

He nods vigorously. "Nutrition!"

"What bizarre creatures you have on this planet," I say. "First spiders, and now... anglerfish? Where does this one live?"

Amara pats my shoulder. "I don't think you'll encounter an anglerfish in the apartment. They live in the ocean."

"Already had a run-in with spiders?" a woman in the circle asks, blowing out smoke. The pipe returns to Amara, and she takes another big whiff of it. "I'm terrified of them. I will scream like a baby if I see one."

I nod in understanding. "They are terrible."

"Is the squirrel or the spider worse?" Amara asks, passing me the pipe.

"The spider is smaller and, thus, worse."

Someone else in the circle snorts. "I wonder what you would think of elephants."

While Amara lights the pipe for me again and I inhale the smoke, my translator supplies me with an image of an enormous beast, gray all over with wrinkles and a long snout that drags on the ground.

"At least you would know it's coming," I say, coughing the smoke out again. "I could hide in Amara's closet."

Everyone laughs, and I'm happy knowing that I did it. My brain feels almost... syrupy, thick. But also sweet, like something I tried called *cotton candy*. I realize I've been smiling widely for some time now, and so is Amara, her hand clasped around my arm as she likes to do. She has so many habits, all of them interesting, most endearing. Even the ones that aren't, like sniffling while we watch a movie instead of blowing her nose because of her allergies, are still cute because they're *hers*.

Still, I often supply her with a box of tissue after an hour has gone by.

I realize I've been lost in thought, and everyone is looking at me expectantly, waiting for an answer.

"Roth'kar, he asked about your cool toothbrush thing?" Amara reminds me gently.

"Oh, yes." I pretend like I didn't miss anything. "You see, it has a sonic vibration that knocks all detritus off of the teeth, and then you simply rinse it out."

"What other cool alien gear do you have?" the man in the top hat asks.

Though they are all strangers, I feel far more confident than I ever have around humans before. All their eyes trained on me, waiting for my answer, pleases me. I was never much of a social being in the Hole, but now I feel happy and bold.

"I have a communicator." I withdraw the tiny device from my pocket. It's small enough so as not to have an input display—it projects one, which it does when I hold it out. All the humans gape and gawk, clearly having never seen anything like it before. I preen.

"That's so cool," Amara says. "You've never even shown it to me."

"It is typically private. But I will share anything you like with you."

"Ooh," says one of the other women in the circle. "He's a good one. You should probably keep him."

Amara giggles and pulls me closer. "Yeah, I think I will."

Though I have been operating under the belief that Amara will want to stay with me after the trial ends, hearing her affirm it so easily, so casually, makes my whole being radiate with joy.

One of the humans asks to see the communicator, so I set it to English and pass it around, and they all marvel at how small it is. I feel so warm in the best way, my arm around Amara, new friends chattering around us.

The humans start pressing buttons on the display, seeing what it does.

"Message from Zono," it reads aloud. Oh, no. I forgot about that.

I try to snatch the communicator back from the human currently examining it, but it's too far away.

"Zono?" Amara asks. "Isn't that one of your friends back on the ship?"

Once again I reach for the communicator, but it's moved on to the next person to look at, and they are too inebriated to notice me trying to recover it.

As a human would say, *fuck.*

The message pops up, displaying in the center of the circle.

"I had a thought," Zono says, the communicator automatically translating him as it reads aloud. *"You should connect me to one of your wife's friends so I can also get out of*

here. Just give them my name! You know I would give you all my chips for a free, easy ticket out of here, too."

Amara is watching, listening, her mouth slowly falling open.

No, no, I can't have her hear this. I reach for the communicator again, desperate to retrieve it before Zono can make it even worse.

"And then when we both have our citizenship, we can leave and go exploring together, Roth'kar! We won't need them anymore. I have been researching Earth, and—"

I finally snatch the communicator from the top hat man and snap it closed. But Amara has already heard Zono's message, and there is nothing I can do to rip the words back out of the air.

"Roth'kar?" she asks, her voice small, painfully small. "What is he talking about?"

"Foolishness." My skin crawls as I shove the communicator back in my pocket. "Zono is an idiot."

Amara takes a step back from me. "You're just here to get your citizenship on Earth?"

Everyone else in the circle is silent. It feels as if the entire planet is turning upside down. I reach for Amara, but then she takes another step back, so I can't touch her.

"You were going to use me?" Her joy is collapsing in on itself, morphing into a devastating sadness. "You only came here to… get away. To escape the Hole. Didn't you? It was never about me."

My mouth opens and closes. It feels like it's full of that other candy, the terrible one. *Toffee.* My lips are stuck as I try to figure out the right words to say. If I lie to her now, again, it will only make this worse.

No, the truth was obvious in Zono's message.

"Yes," I say at last. "I only participated in the Matching Program to get away from *New Droth'ar II*."

Someone in the circle gasps.

"But Amara, I didn't know. I'm sorry. I didn't know you, I didn't know Earth, I didn't understand how wonderful and kind and—"

Amara's face slams closed. It's like a hardness has risen inside her, cold as a stone. Before I've even finished speaking, she turns on her heel and walks back into the house.

CHAPTER NINETEEN

AMARA

I CAN'T BELIEVE IT. I just can't. Everything about this marriage has been a lie since the very beginning. The only reason he came to Earth was to escape the hell he lived in. He never wanted me; I was merely a convenience to get what he needed.

How long was he planning to use me and then leave me? I know I should ask him these questions to his face, but I'm so angry, so betrayed, that I can't even look at him because it burns my soul.

I gave so much of myself to Roth'kar, all while he planned to gallivant off the moment the deed was done. He convinced me he cared for me, that we would be a good pair, just so I wouldn't end it before the thirty days was up.

I can't believe I let him touch me, that I let him *have sex with me*. That I practically cut open my heart and handed him a piece of it when he never intended to do the same.

"Amara!" Roth'kar calls after me as I head into the house, my whole body hot, so hot, my senses on overdrive as I try to process the avalanching heartbreak. "Amara, wait."

I stop and turn to him. "I am leaving." My voice comes out weaker than I intend, but I'm weak, so weak, for him. "I am leaving to go home. I don't want to see you until tomorrow. You can sleep at Marguerite's house—I'll tell her you're staying."

He opens his mouth like he wants to argue, but I ignore him, turning away again so I can go find Marguerite. Roth'kar follows me again.

"Please," he says, reaching for my hand. "Amara, it's not like any of that anymore."

I jerk it away, because just touching him is painful.

"Stop it!" I snap. "Just stop! I can't even look at you! I need to be alone."

When I charge off again, Roth'kar stands still, watching me go.

I'm in tears when I finally find Marguerite. I can barely get the words out, but somehow she's able to discern my meaning, because she pats my shoulder and assures me she'll take care of everything.

All I can do is flee from the house before I break down.

I cry the entire light rail ride home, wishing that Roth'kar was with me, hating that he's not, hating that he lied to me, hating that everything is *wrong*.

He never wanted me. Even now, was he planning to bounce the moment the trial was over? Is everything he ever told me, everything we ever did, even real? Was sleeping with me part of his plan?

The thought absolutely disgusts me, and the moment I'm through the front door of my condo, I get into the shower and scrub myself clean under the hot water. I feel vomit rise in my throat.

He did what he needed to do. He did what was *expected* of him, just like we talked about. I was right.

No, wait, I am going to throw up.

After getting it all out into the toilet, I close the lid and lean my head on it, wet and cold and exhausted. I've gone through some nasty breakups, but nothing has hit me where it hurts quite like this.

Finally, I heave myself off the bathroom floor, towel dry, and head into the bedroom. The sheets and blanket are still a mess from earlier, when I was trying to put on my dress and Roth'kar insisted on taking it off me.

I fall onto the bed, breaking out into sobs all over again. I lie under the blankets that smell like my husband, miserable and sick to my stomach, until I fall asleep.

The next morning, I feel like a cake that got dropped from a twenty-story building. When I slide out of bed, though, I smell bacon fat cooking. Quickly, I throw on my slippers and robe and stumble out into the hallway.

In the kitchen, Roth'kar stands over two hot pans. He turns when I appear.

"I made breakfast," he says carefully. "Plenty of grease. And here's some coffee." I stand there as he pours me a mug from the coffee maker and slides it across the table in my direction.

I know what he's trying to do. It's not worth it. I already went through this entire breakup in my head last night, and while I might be exhausted now, it's because I know the right answer.

"Roth'kar." I sit down at the table, studiously ignoring the coffee.

"Almost done." His tone is almost frantic. "Just a few more minutes."

"Roth'kar."

He gives me a pleading look. "Don't make me leave." He pushes the pans aside and comes to the table, sitting across from me. He reaches for me, but I don't take his outstretched hand. "Please, Amara. It's not because of the Hole. I don't want to leave *you*. I've never felt happiness like I have with you, and—"

"I'm not making you leave."

I say the words strong and hard, so he won't question them.

Roth'kar's antennae lift for a moment from where they've been plastered miserably against his head. "You won't?"

"No. I could never send you back there, even though it didn't work out between us."

"It... didn't?" He searches my face for what I'm saying. "What do you mean, Amara? You're going to stay married to me?"

"Until we sign the documents and make everything official, so you can get residency on Earth."

I hate the words as they come out of my mouth, but it's the right thing to do. I wouldn't be able to live with myself if Roth'kar had to return to the Hole after how terrible it was.

But he can't stay in my house, either. I can't be his wife, knowing what I know now. Not when there's still a chance he would leave me.

Roth'kar's tone is worried as he asks, "And then? After?"

"And then we get divorced, and you can go off and do whatever you want."

His antennae droop, and he lowers his head.

"You'll let me stay here until the paperwork is done, and then you want me to leave."

"Yes."

I'm trying to keep calm, but inside my heart is breaking into pieces all over again. But I deserve more than this. I deserve someone who chose *me*. Who wants *me*.

"It's only a few more days," I point out. "Gazargo comes back on the third."

"Three days." Roth'kar raises those blue eyes to mine, and they are bottomless. "Three days until I have my citizenship."

"And then you can go."

He nods slowly, his hands curled into fists. Then he rises silently from the table, serves the food on two plates, and puts one in front of me. He looks numb as he sits down, and we both eat in silence.

The rest of the day passes much the same: in silence. I deposit Roth'kar's clothes outside the spare room in a neat pile, then go into my own room and shut the door so I can be alone. I lie on my bed, miserable, staring at the wall and wishing everything was different.

When I emerge again, he's taken the clothes away and retreated to his own room.

I make dinner that night, and Roth'kar tries to help, so I let him. I say nothing, and though he glances at me from time to time, he doesn't speak, either.

Over our meal, he says, "Amara, please, let me explain myself."

My response is firm and final. "I think you did already."

He falters. Looking down at his plate, Roth'kar doesn't attempt to make conversation again.

I will give him what he wants. I'll make sure he has everything he needs to build a life for himself. And then we'll wash our hands of each other.

The next morning, I get up early for work, before my alarm has even gone off. When I walk out into the kitchen, Roth'kar is already awake and cooking. He slides a plate of food into my spot at the table.

"So that you have a good day today," he says, by way of explanation.

I don't answer. I can't trust myself to answer without breaking down. His attempt to take care of me, to be kind to me, grates on my nerves. How can he go about this farce still?

After I eat, I throw on my bag and head out the door.

The day is a slog. Kendall knows something is up, and she offers to talk about it, but I'm not ready. I don't know if I'll ever be ready.

SO I MARRIED AN ALIEN

I thought I'd found the love of my life, but I was just a path for him to get what he wanted.

Have things changed since then, like he's arguing? I believe Roth'kar cares about me, yes. But if I asked him point-blank if he still intended on leaving... would I believe his answer? Do I really know his heart?

I don't think I do, not anymore.

That's what hurts the most—how our relationship had blossomed so fully, only for all the trust I had in him to be destroyed. Now, I'm mourning it.

The drive back from work makes me infuriated as other drivers cut in front of me, because an accident has slowed everything down. I just want to slam on my horn and shout at someone. It's all so unfair.

Finally, I'm home, but I dread walking in the front door. Just seeing Roth'kar's face this morning was like a dagger to the chest.

When I finally step inside, I'm greeted by the scent of onions, garlic, and spices. I frown when I spot Roth'kar in the kitchen, wearing my apron, busying about over two pans and a pot on the stove. He turns when I enter, and he offers me a tentative smile.

"Curry?" he asks.

Fuck. He knows I love curry. He knows I'd do anything for it, and I hate that he's trying to buy me back with food.

It's not about whether or not I love him. I'm pretty sure that I do. It's about whether or not I can trust what we've built—and how it feels like our little city of budding love was wiped out in a tidal wave.

"Roth'kar, I'm sorry."

He turns his head again. "For what?"

"This is pointless. It's not about forgiveness. You can't just undo what's been done. Everything between us is based on a lie, and I don't think I can ever trust you again."

His antennae flatten, and he turns back to the food. He doesn't speak for a long time, and I think he's not going to answer me at all until he says, "I am not trying to buy your forgiveness, Amara."

He serves rice in bowls, and then dishes out the curry over it, topping it off with yogurt and cilantro before bringing it to the table. He sets one in front of me, then seats himself on the other side of the table.

"I am trying to take care of you. That is my job, as your husband. To take care of you and protect you, even if you don't want me to do it. And I'll do it as long as I can, until you make me leave."

CHAPTER TWENTY

ROTH'KAR

I'VE NEVER FELT an agony as excruciating as seeing how badly I destroyed everything with Amara. It seethes under the surface of my skin, knowing how I've hurt her and that there is no way I can fix it.

Even in her sadness and her fury, she is generous, wanting to complete the marriage so that I can stay on Earth. Perhaps that injures me most of all—that she will do this to help me even when it hurts her.

I want to blame Zono, but it's not his fault. I was the one who lied, she is right. I used the Matching Program to escape, not caring who was on the other end. And now that's caught up to me.

Things may be different for me now, but she has no reason to believe that. She doesn't know what's in my soul.

As much as I want to fight, Amara has closed her doors to me. She has locked me away, steeled her heart to me, and I'm not sure that any amount of fighting would break through.

And so, I will simply do what I can to make sure that, when she asks me to leave, I'll have done the best I could to be her mate. I don't know what will come after when she files for a divorce.

That word makes me shiver.

Only two more days until Gazargo returns for our signatures, and Amara marries me—just for me to lose her right after.

That night, she retires to her room early, and I sit on the couch simply thinking, wishing I knew how to fix this. When I finally go to bed, I'm exhausted, too tired to even attend to my hungry culans. They don't understand why I'm not with Amara, sunk inside her while I kiss her soft lips.

I prepare breakfast again in the morning, which Amara eats without speaking. Once she's left for work, I take down the Halloween decorations, dread building in my belly for tomorrow. That's when Amara and I will sign our names on the tablet to officially be married—a marriage I will never get to enjoy.

Afterward, I decide to head to the park. Perhaps the falling leaves will spark an idea and give me some solution to my problem, if there is one.

Sylvia and her daughter, Izzy, are playing on the playground when I arrive. Izzy runs over, and it is probably the one bright point in my day when she skids to a halt in front of me, buzzing with questions. We begin our walk, and I answer her as best I can.

While Izzy is distracted by a dog coming the other way, Sylvia tips her head in my direction. "You seem sad today, Roth'kar."

I can't possibly express what I really feel with words, the bottomless pain I feel knowing what's coming, so I simply nod.

"What happened? I thought things were going well with the wife?"

I stuff my lower hands in the pocket of my jeans, a habit I've picked up since living on Earth. My other pair of arms cross over my chest protectively. "She has asked me to leave."

Sylvia's taken aback. "Really? Why? That's awful."

"I made a mistake when this all began. I came here under false pretenses. I lied to her."

There, I've said it. And knowing Amara now, knowing how she is always honest and trusting, I also understand why it cut her deep.

"I'm surprised to hear that." Sylvia interrupts herself to call Izzy, who has now run off into the grass to investigate the duck pond. "That doesn't sound like you."

I shrug. "It is the truth. And now my wife wants nothing more to do with me."

"Well, if you need somewhere to stay, we have a couch." She sighs. "That's so sad. You seemed like a good match."

"We are," I say firmly. "I believe that we would have been a very good pair. We complement each other well, and we have... a certain attraction to one another."

Her brows draw together. "Then why does it sound like you've accepted that it's over?"

"Because she has made that clear to me."

And I don't want to encroach on Amara further when she has already given me so much, and once we separate, she plans to give me more to help me get on my own two feet. It is the worst outcome, surely, but there's nothing I can do to change it now that she's made up her mind.

I have learned much about my wife in the last few days. I thought her sweet and soft, but she is also fierce to protect herself.

"So you're just going to roll over?" Sylvia asks.

"Roll over?"

"You're going to roll over like a dog and let it happen."

"I will *never* be like a dog." I cross my arms even tighter across my chest.

"Then don't act like one," Sylvia says as Izzy comes running back from examining the ducks. "She must care about you."

"She did." I feel certain about this. "But not anymore."

"Surely she still does. Those feelings don't just go away overnight."

Little does she know about Amara. Her devotion and love are just as deep as her hurt.

Sylvia pats my arm. "Put up a fight. Don't let her go. Figure out how to get through to her, or you'll regret it for the rest of your life."

"I don't have a life without her," I say, without realizing the words have left my lips. "She is the only thing in the world that has ever mattered to me."

It's true, now that I've said it aloud. Never have I cared for someone like Amara. Never have I wanted for someone's happiness like Amara's. And that is why, if she thinks she would be better without me, it's my job to let her have that.

"What are you talking about?" says Izzy, taking her mother's hand.

"Roth'kar's wife. She's mad at him. What do you think he should do to make it up to her?"

Izzy taps her chin. "Flowers are boring. You have to show you're really sorry."

Sylvia nods in agreement.

"What does your wife like?" Izzy asks. "You should get her something you know she really, really wants. Something that would make her happy again."

I don't think anything I gave her would clear away the stain of what I've done.

"Maybe something that she really *needs*," Sylvia attempts. "You know her well now, don't you? What is missing in her life? Show her you understand her."

Show her I understand her. I do understand Amara, I believe. Perhaps too well, and that's how I know that no matter what, it won't work.

But there might be something I can do to make her life better even after I'm gone, and that is the best I can do.

I explain my idea to Sylvia and she agrees to it. That afternoon, she drives me to the animal shelter, Izzy bouncing in the back seat.

Amara has told me many times about her cat, Elvis, who she had for most of her adult life. He meant the world to her, and when he passed away, she couldn't contain her loneliness any longer. It was the trigger, more or less, for her applying to the Matching Program.

I know she will be lonely after I leave, so I'll do this to ensure that someone can be there for her when she's by herself again.

Even as we approach the shelter, I can't mistake the sound of barking dogs. I shudder, but Sylvia encourages me on as we walk inside the building.

There are cats everywhere. In cages, walking around on the countertop, sleeping in beds on the floor and climbing carpeted structures. Cats, cats, and more cats. I have my pick, it would seem.

We approach the front desk, where a receptionist has a very tiny dog on her lap. I jump back, but it barely lifts its head as she pets it.

"An alien!" She grins in that wide, brilliant way humans do. "Wow. Cool."

"Hello." I offer my hand to her to shake, and a little perplexed, she accepts. "I am here to take a cat home to my wife."

Her brows rise. "Oh! You're looking for a new furry friend, huh? Well, you came to the right place." She stands up, still holding the tiny dog. "Sarah! This guy wants a cat. Can you help him out?"

Another woman appears, older but somehow more spritely, and she hurries over.

"We have many to choose from," she says in a smooth voice. "What are you looking for in a new forever friend?"

"He will be my wife's, erm, forever friend."

She cocks a brow. "Oh, okay. Well, what is she looking for?"

I have to think hard about this. She needs someone sturdy and reliable. Someone who will curl up next to her at night, and who will have plenty of love to dole out.

"An affectionate cat," I say at last.

"We've got plenty of snugglers." She points out a few cats in the main room before leading us back to the "cat room." It's swarming with the small animals. One of them immediately walks up to me and sniffs my leg. I reach down to pet it cautiously, and it lifts its head into my hand. It is brown all over with black striping and is very handsome.

"That's Bernard. He's a good guy. Older than some of the others and definitely cuddly. He loves attention."

Yes. That's what Amara will need. A good, older male that will cuddle. And hopefully keep the spiders away.

"I choose him, then." I pick up the little animal carefully, and he has no complaints as I cradle him in my arms. After a while of petting his head, his body starts making a low rumbling noise. "That's odd. He is vibrating."

"Purring! He likes you." Sarah looks pleased. "I guess he picked you back. Want me to start the paperwork?"

I nod, holding Bernard close to my chest. I think he will be just what Amara needs.

It is a sharp, smooth piece of scrap metal, driven right into my heart.

Sylvia drops me off at home after I have secured the things the cat will need. It took all my remaining *bucks* to buy the litter box, bed, and food, but Bernard should have everything a cat would want, including a toy at the end of a string.

Bernard is happy to be carried, and when released inside Amara's house, he starts sniffing everything. Before long, he is settled on the couch—not where I had intended, given I purchased him his own bed—but I get the sense I cannot tell Bernard what to do.

I start on dinner, a recipe I have not seen Amara make, but I think it will work given what I've learned about human food. Amara especially loves peppers, so I will use many of the mild ones. I also make her favorite rice to go with it.

I turn when I hear her footsteps outside the front door. The knob turns and the door opens, and Amara comes inside with her shoulders tight.

"Welcome home," I say. She stiffens even further. I know my presence here hurts her. "I have a surprise."

Her brows knit together. "Why? Don't get me things. I don't want—"

But I am already picking up Bernard and holding him up for her. Her eyes go round, and she takes a few hesitant steps toward us.

"Is that a cat, Roth'kar?" she asks, though it is obvious to both of us that it is.

"I am not trying to buy your affection." I feel this is important to clarify. "This is not a gift so that you'll reconsider. But I worry about… when you are alone."

Her frown gets deeper. "You don't need to worry about me."

"But I will!" I grit my teeth together. "I will. But if

Bernard is with you, then I know you won't be alone when I am gone."

Most unexpectedly, Amara's eyes grow wet and shining. She takes another step closer, and I offer Bernard to her, who is purring in my arms.

She takes him uncertainly, but he is already content, curling up in the crook of her elbow. Tears stream from her eyes as she looks down at the furry animal, and then she hugs him, clutching him close to her chest.

I think it was a good gift.

CHAPTER TWENTY-ONE

AMARA

ROTH'KAR GOT ME A CAT. So I wouldn't be lonely without him.

How fucked up is that? He's looking out for me even when he won't be around. It's just like him, too, in the most painful way possible. He has accepted where we are, and what I want, but worries about me still.

He's not concerned about how he'll continue, but how I will.

I squeeze sweet Bernard, and he doesn't seem to mind. His purring feels calming against my chest as my heart beats wildly.

"Roth'kar." The word comes out strangled. "You didn't have to do this."

"I know how much it hurt when you lost Elvis," he says. "I don't want you to be by yourself."

The tears are rolling in fat drops down my cheeks. Oh,

my alien husband. I love him so much that it's physically painful.

Could I really just watch him walk away? I might die inside.

"You have to tell me..." I can barely speak, but I try anyway. "You have to tell me things are different now. That you're not just using me because it sucks too much to go home."

Roth'kar gently takes Bernard from my arms and sets him on the couch. Measured and even, as always, my husband takes my hands in his lower ones, then sets the upper pair on my shoulders.

"Amara."

Just his touch makes me shiver all over. I've needed him so badly, it feels like delicious fire on my skin.

"I have seen many romantic movies now," he says, looking into me with those deep blue eyes as he speaks. "And the thing that fixes things is when one of them says, 'I love you,' and then everything is right again. As true as it is—that I do love you—I know that will not fix things here. It won't change what I did or how I came into this marriage."

I nod weakly. It won't be solved like that, but hearing the words sparks joy inside me, too.

"What I can promise you is that I will always, always be at your side, Amara, as long as you want me there. I did not know what I'd find on Earth, and you are beyond my most beautiful dream. All I desire is to see you happy, whether that is with or without me. But if I may speak the truth..."

The tears are coming so fast that all I can do is nod and

try not to sob. That is what I've always wanted—someone at my side, someone to grow old with me.

"I think you would be happier with me," Roth'kar says, pushing some hair back behind my ear. "I think that over many years, I will prove to you I was the right choice, regardless of how we began. That the little alien had some sense when he put us together."

I know that he's right, that the matchmaker did one thing correctly. Gazargo must have known I needed someone steadfast, someone who would hold me down to Earth in a warm embrace.

"Yeah," is all I can manage. "I know I would be sadder without you."

"Then please, don't ask me to leave." Roth'kar gently takes my chin and tilts my face up, so his lips are only inches from mine. "Let me take care of you. Let me cook meals and rub your feet and go dancing with you. Let me be your husband, and I promise I will never let you down again."

It's everything I've ever wanted, everything I'd ever dreamed of having for myself. And Roth'kar wants to give all of it to me.

When I stumble forward into his arms, he catches me easily. All four of his hands wrap around me, drawing me in close, cradling me against his chest. One strokes the back of my head as I cry against him, letting out everything I've been holding in.

"Please, stay with me," I whimper into his wet shirt. Roth'kar squeezes me tighter, kissing the top of my head over and over.

"I will. Always."

I sniffle, lifting my head to glance around him at where

Bernard is sleeping again on the couch. "I still want the cat, though. He's staying."

My alien smiles down at me. "Deal."

Then the oven timer beeps. Roth'kar gently releases me and offers me a tentative smile.

"Dinner?"

The food is incredible, which is shocking given Roth'kar wasn't following a recipe, nor imitating the way I've cooked in the past. The meal is something all his own, and he seems proud as I devour it. But that's also because I just cried so hard I'm starving.

We feed Bernard his wet food, and Roth'kar shows me where he stationed the litter box. I'm excited to have a cat again—and I'm glad we can share the experience. Roth'kar clearly adores Bernard, and I feel like our little family is complete when the cat crawls up his chest and falls asleep there while we talk.

And we do talk through everything, from when Roth'kar first learned about the Galactic Matching Program to the call he had with Zono.

"I should have said something to you then," he says. "But I didn't want to lose what I had with you."

He twines our fingers together while he pets Bernard with his other hand, the one that's not cradling the cat like a baby. Still amazing to me how he can be so many places at once.

"I hope we can tell each other everything from now on." I look down at our linked hands, his purple-blue fingers interlaced with my brown ones. "Even the stuff that sucks."

Roth'kar nods. "Most assuredly."

Then he puts the cat to bed, and I lead him along behind me to the bedroom.

I missed him too much to wait. The moment we're in the door, I have him pushed up against it, grabbing the bottom hem of his shirt and pulling it up over his arms. He helps me until his big chest is bare, and I'm enamored with him all over again.

I nearly tear off my own shirt and then stumble over my jeans as I try to pull them down. Roth'kar reaches out and steadies me, all while he takes off his belt and pants. Then we're standing there, naked, and his culans are reaching out to me. I return the touch, and they clasp around my fingers. Roth'kar groans when I wrap my other hand around the base and squeeze.

But I know what I want, and I want it now. Those lovely little ridges will feel exquisite. And I want to be close to him again, to feel consumed by him, to merge ourselves once more.

As if he can read my mind, Roth'kar reaches under my ass with his lower arms and lifts me up, propping my back against the door. While he's holding me that way, one of his other hands wanders downward, between my legs. He teases my clit and plucks at my nipple at the same time, and I'll never get tired of how dexterous he is with all four appendages.

"I need to be inside you," Roth'kar murmurs into my ear, adjusting his lower arms so I'm perched right where I need to be for his cock to slide in.

"Please."

His culans snap together, tines interlocking, and the tapered tip pushes through. And oh fuck, how good it feels to be spread open again. I cling to him, arms wrapped around his neck as he halts partway in, breathing heavily.

"You are divine." He captures my chin with one hand and presses his lips to mine. His tongue comes out to play while he pulls out slightly, then slides in even farther.

Being together again, like this—there is no greater pleasure. And my husband, who cares for me like no one ever has, who comes along on all my adventures with me, who lets me be what I am. I'm eternally grateful for him.

Roth'kar grunts as he seats himself fully, and I sense when the tines along his culans shudder and tremble. He withdraws only a fraction, then sinks in again, searching for where to best tease me. He is as attentive of a partner as he is a lover, seeking out what I like most and then pursuing it with determination.

Soon I'm trembling, crying his name, arms curled tight around his neck to hold him close to me as he rhythmically pumps his hips, the door creaking with every thrust. Within only a few moments I can't hold it in any longer, and when my orgasm hits me, my legs clamp tight around his waist and my vision goes white. Roth'kar's culans flutter inside me, and he lets out a shout of his own as he shoves himself deep.

Eventually, Roth'kar stumbles back to the bed with me in his lap, his cock still inside me. He nuzzles my face, then lies back while holding me tight against him.

"Please sleep with me," I say, stroking his cheek. "Here in our bed."

He nods, smiling as he traces the shape of my hip. "Of course. I would like nothing more."

The following day is our official wedding, and I wake up with butterflies in my belly. I ask Fiona if she'll be our witness, and she happily agrees to come along.

Fiona waits patiently in a folding chair while Gazargo draws up the agreements to sign. A tablet rests on the chair beside her with a video feed of my mother at a cruise ship bar, a drink in her hand.

"Hey, Amara!" Mom calls, lifting her cup. "I'm sorry I couldn't make it, but I'm so proud of you! Even though you're not wearing a wedding dress!"

I roll my eyes and wave at her.

"Love you, Mom."

There are no more vows to make, but Roth'kar surprises everyone by saying, "I want to say my commitments."

Gazargo frowns. "You already did those a month ago."

"They were not true to my heart."

Roth'kar takes my hands in his, and with a grunt of annoyance, the little Frahma gets out of the way.

"Amara," Roth'kar begins, holding my gaze. "I promise to always be honest with you. To open my heart to you and hold yours tight in my hands. I promise to care for you, to protect you, to share my life with you until death do us part."

I'm surprised at the last bit.

"Even then," he says with a chuckle, "I will probably

still be watching over you, just to make sure you don't trip on a crack or wander down a dark alley."

I can't help it. I throw my arms around him, and he embraces me in return, squeezing me tight. Then he leans back so he can kiss me on the lips.

"Ahem," Gazargo says after we've been making out a little too long. "Can we get on to the signatures? Then I can file the paperwork for Roth'kar's permanent visa."

We finally pull apart, and Gazargo sets the tablet down in front of us. We each sign our names, and then the deal is done.

We're married.

Fiona stands up, clapping wildly as we kiss again. Gazargo rolls his eyes as he takes the tablet away, but I think the little wrinkly alien is smiling.

"Another successful match," he says to himself as he waves goodbye to us.

We're done. All the Ts have been crossed, the Is dotted, and we're ready for our happily ever after together.

CHAPTER TWENTY-TWO

ROTH'KAR

WE CAN'T DRIVE BACK to the condo fast enough. We drop off Fiona, who gives Amara and I both big hugs.

"Congratulations," she says. Then she smacks me on the shoulder playfully. "Take care of my best friend, okay?"

I agree to do exactly that, and she gives me a nod of approval.

Finally, we're home. Bernard is waiting at the door for us, and Amara scoops him up, kissing his forehead as she holds him close. I slide my arms around her waist from behind, nuzzling her throat and whispering in her ear exactly what I want to do to her. With a wide grin, she sets Bernard down in his cat bed and allows me to lead her to our bedroom.

When I have Amara's clothes off, she is already wet for me, but I plan to show her far greater pleasures. I kiss her clit, lapping it and sucking on it while I pump my fingers in and out of her tight channel, driving her moans ever louder. My culans are clasped tight and full of blood, ready to please her.

Amara crests, her legs shivering and her thighs pressing together around my head, but I don't relent. I plan to make my wife orgasm many, many more times tonight.

When I've nursed a second finish out of her, Amara lies there, boneless and gasping. I lie beside her and turn her gently so we are on our sides, her back facing my front. Obediently, she lifts one of her thighs, and I pull her hips toward me until I'm positioned just right.

As always, she is perfectly shaped for me, accepting me easily into her body. But I go slow anyway, only sinking in an inch before pulling back, giving her a taste but nothing more. She is so deliciously tight and warm, it is difficult for me to rein myself in, but I manage to remain shallow, teasing her until she's squirming and trying to bring in more of me.

"Roth'kar," she moans. "Please, I need you."

I cannot bear to deny her, so I push in the rest of the way, demanding her small channel open for me. And open it does, welcoming me in, squeezing so deliciously around me that I bite my lip to hold off on coming too soon.

I keep my thrusts slow, building Amara up higher and higher, relishing each of her sweet cries. I want all of them.

Soon, she is close, shaking and shivering with every pump of my hips. I reach around her thigh to strum her clit while I make love to her, and Amara tightens up all around me.

"Oh, fuck." She cries out her bliss, and I shove into her

faster, spinning her climax up and then reveling in it as it shatters her.

That delicious clenching is all it takes to drag me over the edge. Both my culans release, and I bury myself inside her one final time as they spill everything. Soon my spend is leaking out of her, and Amara is panting, her body trembling from the force of it.

Eventually, I withdraw and wrap her up in my arms, cradling her body against mine.

"I can't wait to do this for the rest of our lives," I tell her, kissing her cheek, her neck, her shoulder. "Forever."

"Forever," she whispers back, settling into me. "The best I could have hoped for."

Now that I have my permanent visa, I can, at last, apply for a job. The convenience store on the corner is happy to take me, and I schedule my shifts for when Amara is at work. This way, I can contribute to our household while still getting home in time to prepare dinner. At the gift boutique down the street, I use my first paycheck to pick out some trinkets to add to the apartment, ones that I feel represent me. My favorite is a small, square painting of a cat. Amara is immensely pleased with my choices and helps me pick out where they should go in the condo.

I buy many recipe books so I can make even more interesting foods for her from all over the world. We discuss saving up for a honeymoon so that, perhaps, we could explore some of the places where my favorite cuisines originate. I am curious to see more of Earth and all it has to offer. Amara shows me photographs of huge snow-capped mountains and sandy beaches beside a vast blue-green ocean. It is a mythic thing to me, a body of water that encompasses most of the planet, so we arrange our itineraries to go to a country called Mexico—the home of some of my favorite spicy foods.

We entertain sometimes and have our friends over for dinner. They feel like *our* friends now, Marguerite and Fiona and Kendall. Even Marguerite, who gave me a firm dressing-down when I hurt Amara, has forgiven me. I think all it took was a good enchilada and a stiff margarita to show her I am truly a good match for her best friend.

And then, the time has come at last for our honeymoon. It's a long journey to Mexico, and I marvel from my window seat on the plane at how much of Earth there is to see. Soon, the ocean appears, and it is as majestic as I imagined it would be.

My translator works with the local language, which is a boon. I have purchased a swimsuit, and the first thing we do is head down to the beach to get wet in the ocean.

I am surprised to discover that the water is not drinkable, but terribly salty. Amara laughs as I spit it out, horrified.

"Water that cannot be drunk?" I grumble. What a terrible taunt.

"Yep! And it covers seventy percent of the planet." Amara sets down a towel on the sand, a substance which is very foreign and squishy under my feet. I find that even though I attempt to remain on the towel, the sand gets everywhere, sticking to my skin, my clothes, even my culans inside my shorts. How did it get there?

I am not sure how I feel about the beach, though my

wife seems to enjoy lying out in the sun with her sunglasses on, soaking up powerful UV rays. I make sure to apply sunscreen to her often so she doesn't burn, and do the same for myself.

Then, after we have eaten so much Mexican food we feel close to bursting, we shower off all the remaining sand. After we've toweled ourselves dry, I pull Amara to the bed, and she giggles as she falls onto it.

I crouch over her, my culans already swelling and eager to please. I lower my hips to hers so they can reach for her, teasing her clit and her sweet pussy. She eagerly bucks against me, ready for me to take her.

But I have a plan. There is something Amara particularly enjoys, and I made sure to bring plenty of lube so that I can please her in every way. First, though, I need to taste her. I want to make her gush.

My fingers and tongue know exactly what to do with her sweet body to make her whine. Since I plan on taking my time, I nurse her close to her finish before relenting, letting her come down before bringing her back to the peak again.

"Roth'kar!" she begs, shivering all over. "Please!"

I curl my fingers inside her and tease her favorite place as I devour her clit, and it's easy to make her cry out. Liquid drips down my hand, and I know that she's ready for me.

"Get on your knees," I instruct her. Amara is still shivering from her climax as she rolls over, then lifts her ass in the air in front of me. Her release shines in the light as I guide my lower culans inside her, then retrieve the bottle of lube.

Amara turns her head, her eyes wide. "Oh?"

"Oh yes," I affirm, coating my finger in the oily liquid, then running it over the tighter ring of muscle around her ass. This is not the first time I've made use of both her entrances, so my upper culans easily slips inside, and my wife moans with her face in the pillow. I widen her for me, thrusting gently and slowly as I prepare her.

"Oh!" Amara cries out as I push in again. I know to go slow now, so I only bury it a fraction of the way inside her before withdrawing again. Her whole body trembles under me as I sink it in a second time, deeper.

"Roth'kar," she moans, clenching the pillow. "Please, more!"

Good. She is ready for me.

This time I slide all the way in, both culans enveloped in her warmth. It won't take much to send her over the edge like this, so I go slow and steady, building her up one snap of my hips at a time. Amara's voice rises in pitch as my own orgasm threatens to overtake me, but I maintain my pace, pushing it back. She clenches even tighter around me, strangling my culans in the most pristine and delightful way.

"Amara," I murmur, leaning down over her back to stroke her hair. "My love, my wife."

That's all it takes. I slam into her as her shout fills the room, and her grip around my culans is so powerful that it practically rips my own climax out of me.

I groan as I fill her, shoving in again and again to draw out her pleasure. Amara keens as my spend spills out of her, dripping down onto the hotel bed.

"Oh, fuck," she moans, her knees finally giving out. I lie atop her, my elbows keeping me from crushing her.

Gently, I work my culans free, and Amara whimpers again as I withdraw from her ass.

I collapse beside her, then roll her up into my arms.

"You know I will always love you, don't you?" I ask her, kissing the crown of her head.

She snuggles even closer. "I know. And you're mine. All mine."

I chuckle. "I am indeed."

It's not long before she falls asleep, curled up against me.

Forever with my sweet human is the greatest gift I could have possibly received.

THANK YOU FOR READING!

I hope you liked Roth'kar and Amara's story. If you enjoyed this book, please consider leaving a review! Reviews help indie authors like me to find new readers.

JOIN MY NEWSLETTER!

For all the latest regarding books, and to get a FREE Trollkin Lovers novella, join my newsletter!

www.LyonneRiley.com

ACKNOWLEDGMENTS

I would like to thank everyone involved in helping me through the process of putting out this book, especially my Tumblr followers, who inspired it. I can't say enough how much I appreciate the help of the people around me —especially Amber, who told me I could do this in the first place.

Huge thank you to all of my friends for encouraging me to write this book, and Theresa for capturing Roth'kar and Amara so well. To my critique partners, who gave me phenomenal editorial feedback: You all make this possible. And of course, my amazing spouse, who has always supported my dreams—and given me lots of inspiration for my characters' sexy adventures.

I couldn't have done this without the expertise of my fellow self-published romance authors. Thank you for inviting me into your circles and helping me through this process.

And thank you to my readers, who gave this book a shot.

ABOUT THE AUTHOR

Lyonne Riley published her first book at age five, which was written on tiny sheets of notebook paper, and she insisted on giving a copy to everyone she knew. She's been writing ever since, from fan fiction in her teen years to original fiction as an adult. After a stint in traditional publishing, she discovered what she truly wanted to write: very smutty stories about monsters and the little humans they worship.

Now she lives in the middle of nowhere with her dogs and spouse, writing sexy fairy tales.

www.ingramcontent.com/pod-product-compliance
Lightning Source LLC
Chambersburg PA
CBHW060559190726
48283CB00003B/1080

9 781917 032902